LYN MOORE

Madhouse Promenade

LYNMOORE
HOUSE

First published by Lynmoore House LLC 2024

Copyright © 2024 by Lyn Moore

All rights reserved. No part of this publication may be reproduced, stored or transmitted in any form or by any means, electronic, mechanical, photocopying, recording, scanning, or otherwise without written permission from the publisher. It is illegal to copy this book, post it to a website, or distribute it by any other means without permission.

First edition

ISBN: 979-8-9889684-3-6

Illustration by Guilherme Pulga

It will get better

1

The subject entered our home as desolate as the one before him. What brought him to this place could be as small as a splinter or possess the width of time. Human suffering, we have found, is seldom confined to the breadth of the matter. They pay no mind to what it could be, only to what it is to themselves, regardless of whether the sum, or the frequency, the same plight might be found in another.

The light was bright enough to notice through his eyelids, heavy and closed. Ian felt the raw scraping of his throat as he swallowed, the pain in the back of his hand radiating when he shifted positions. He opened his eyes, fluttering against the fluorescents overhead.

A hospital room. One bed, one window, dark against the night sky. He breathed in slowly, looking for the pain point in his hand, noticing the needle trailing back to an IV drip. He exhaled just as slowly and closed his eyes, beckoning the drug-induced sleep to take him back.

He woke again to the sound of someone in his room, the narrow window this time bright with morning sun. The nurse, a middle-aged woman in light scrubs, checked his IV before noticing he was awake.

"How are you feeling?" she asked.

"What time is it?" Ian replied.

She begrudgingly looked at her watch. "Fifteen 'til eleven."

Ian blinked repeatedly, still adjusting to the light. He kicked the covers from his legs, cool air rushing to meet his sweat-soaked skin, unveiling the gray socks he wore. Ian pressed one foot over the other, felt the pattern of dots glued to the underside. He knew where he was, and it was the last place he wanted to be.

"What day?" he asked.

"Thursday," she said. "We don't have an emergency contact on file for you. Have anyone you want us to call?"

No, he didn't. Two days. He had been there two days, his last memory being in a house that was no longer his. When he had laid down on the bed, waiting. Ian took in another deep breath, thankful no one else would know.

"I want to leave."

The nurse picked up the clipboard at the foot of his bed. "You're on a mandatory hold for another sixty-one hours, or until after you see Dr. Bardot."

"Who is that?" he asked.

"Our resident psychiatrist."

Ian sighed. "If I was going to try again, do you think a few hours and a psychiatrist would stop me?"

"That's the law, sir." She sounded almost bored, as if she had this discussion multiple times a day. If it had just worked, he wouldn't be here, wouldn't have to deal with this. Ian thought he had taken enough not to wake up. He'd hoped so.

"Then I'll see the psychiatrist," Ian said. Whatever would get him discharged the quickest.

The nurse gave a knowing smirk and left the room, only to return moments later. "There's an opening at 11 a.m."

"In ten minutes?" Ian asked, remembering the time she had just given him.

1

"Tomorrow morning."

He sat up in bed, his voice rising with him to a level he immediately regretted. "That's a full day from now," he said. The sore throat would have come from the tube they had shoved down it to pump his stomach. It had happened to him once before, but that time was a mistake in college and for something far less threatening—alcohol poisoning.

"And yet still shorter than sixty-one hours."

He looked around in defeat, but did not find what he sought. "Who found me?"

"Sheriff's office," she replied, clipboard still in hand and taking note of various readings from the monitor at his bedside. "A deputy came to enforce the eviction, apparently saw you through a window."

"Did I have anything on me?" he asked noncommittally.

She turned to meet his eye. "You mean the drugs you hadn't yet inhaled, or your wallet?"

He stared back. "Phone."

She hummed her disapproval, leaned down to his bedside table, and pulled out a large plastic bag. He took it from her. His wallet, phone, charger, and ring of now useless keys inside. Through the thick plastic, Ian could tell his phone was dead and decided to keep it that way.

✥

Despite the late hour of the morning, Ian yawned in the slow-moving hospital elevator. His morphine drip long worn off, he found the elusive sleep of the past year to have returned.

The elevator doors opened from one white and beige hall to another, climbing their way to the administrative floor, nurses coming and going while an orderly guided his way. Exiting, they stopped in a waiting area just outside a placard reading *Dr. Bardot*, followed by a number of indecipherable medical abbreviations. The orderly knocked and took a seat, reaching for a magazine on the low centerpiece table.

Moments later the door opened to a mid-forties brunette, eye level to Ian. She carried a consistent deadpan expression, one of neutrality rather than unfriendliness.

"My 11 o'clock, I presume," she said, turning to take note of his chaperone, who nodded in turn. "Come in."

Her office was larger than the waiting room, while keeping its intimacy. Windows lined the left wall, a long paper-covered desk in front of it. Plush open seating to its side, split by another short table, and a beige rug tying it all together.

She motioned for him to sit, following suit herself, not sitting at the desk but in the chair opposite, and pulled a folder from the table between them onto her lap. Ian absent-mindedly thought it must be a therapist ploy. A prop, as he hadn't been here long enough to have even a few pieces of paper on him, let alone a full folder's worth.

"Why can't you sleep?" Dr. Bardot asked, abruptly.

Ian peered up from the carpet, meeting her eyes. He knew he must have bags under them. The burning of sleeplessness told him they'd be red too.

"The fluorescent lights," he lied, looking up toward the same long-tubed fixtures so familiar over his hospital bed.

Dr. Bardot held his gaze when it returned, an ever-so-slight smile rising to his words. "I'm not sure that's the truth," she said.

Ian didn't respond, turning his head to look out the window. It was a better view than he had from the first-floor patient's room. The cold of winter had set in; even at a distance from the glass he could feel the incessant chill radiating from beyond. All he had to do was get through this meeting. If he could just get through it, he could leave. Go home. Wherever home was.

"What led you to your attempt, Ian?" she asked, cutting off his daydream.

Ian huffed a laugh of dissent.

1

"I don't see what's funny."

"*My attempt,*" he mocked. "I tried to kill myself and you call it *my attempt*, like I failed a competition."

"Why do you want to kill yourself?" she asked, not rising to the bait.

Ian found himself content that she didn't. He didn't want to argue. But it was better than being pitied. He couldn't answer her question. He wanted to. He wanted to say that he didn't; that he wanted to live. That he wanted things to go back to normal, that this wasn't him.

But his mouth wouldn't move. It wouldn't give him the energy to spout hope.

"Was it the divorce?" she prodded, holding up a piece of paper from the file in her lap.

Ian met her gaze again, his eyes narrowing and dropping to the folder he wrongly assumed a prop.

"When a person is deemed gravely disabled, a threat to others, or, in your case, a threat to themselves, the seventy-two-hour hold is accompanied by personal information from the state, used to determine the individual's social, legal, financial, and medical situation," Dr. Bardot said.

Ian felt the color drain from his face, the cold seeping in further.

"I won't deny you've had a difficult time. I am not here to judge, I'm here to solve problems." She held up the documents that summarized his life. A folder no more than a few centimeters thick and nothing but words and numbers. Bank balances. Job history. An eviction notice. A divorce filing, he was sure. "This list is nothing more than a list of problems," she finished.

Ian said nothing, the initial worry of his exposed life turning to disdain, heat flushing his face, filling the void of winter. How easily words are said. She spoke as if reading his file plunged her to the depths of his past, to his pain. What it meant to live those failures. Ian didn't know where to begin, to show her how little she knew.

"I need to know how you view these problems, Ian; how you think they happened."

"I thought we were here to see what *you* think?"

"I am not a therapist; I'm a psychiatrist. I'm here to evaluate your mental state to diagnose and treat the underlying conditions. However, I will tell you what I think if you agree to do the same."

Ian stayed quiet, but nodded. She responded by raising her eyebrows in challenge.

"*Yes*. Agreed," he emphasized, and her expression relaxed to her calm neutrality.

She looked down at the folder, flipping through briefly before beginning, "I think positive momentum departed your life a long time ago. That a string of unfortunate outcomes has left you in belief that things will either never get better, or you don't want to wait for them to."

Ian shifted in his seat, growing uncomfortable.

"I think," she hesitated, "You need something to go right, to prove it still can."

What could he say? These were just words to him. Empty hopes of an outsider who didn't know him and offered no ability for change.

"Your turn," was all she said into the quiet.

Ian took a deep breath. "I think that sounds like a lot of work, for an outcome you can't deliver," he said.

"Give us the opportunity to try."

Puzzlement crossed his face before she continued. "In recent years, this hospital has operated a communal assistance program, offering shelter, food, clothing, and even career training for those in need. These resources are yours to use if you're willing to meet the guidelines."

"And what would those be?"

"Simple things," she said. "You must actively look for work. Pass routine drug tests, and meet with a state-sponsored counselor on a

1

regular basis."

The last words hung in the air. Ian could have sworn they were said with a slight inflection. "Let me guess..." he trailed off.

"I would be your counselor, yes."

Ian breathed in heavily while thinking. He had options, though none he was willing to lean on. His parents, mere minutes away for an entire year, yet unaware of how dire his life had become. He could call them back, tell them about how he lost his job. How he lost the house. How things with Laura ended. He still wouldn't admit to trying to end his life. They didn't need to know about that.

There was his brother, Dean, with a wife and two toddlers. Or they were toddlers the last he had seen them. The youngest wouldn't even know his name. Ian had barely talked to Dean these past months, mostly lying when they did. Neither of them were to blame for that; they both had their own life events to deal with and didn't reach out as often as they should. Even if they were close once, Ian knew his brother didn't need the added burden.

Then there were his friends. His old friends, he assumed.

"What if I don't want the state's help?" he asked.

"Depends. Do you intend to make another attempt on your life?"

"I don't know," he said after a pause. The most truthful thing he'd said so far.

It was now her turn to pause, and he was thankful she responded as truthfully. "It would depend on your psych evaluation. If you were no longer suspected to be an immediate threat to yourself, you could leave of your own will." She held there for a moment. "If that is not the outcome of the evaluation, the state would step in regardless. And I'm afraid it won't come with such luxuries."

☦

One house remained in the hospital's living assistance program, and Ian stood on the front steps of the too large and too dark dwelling.

Painted dark gray with a black roof and black-rimmed windows to match, without a light to be seen. It could've fit a family, if one would consider living here. A sparse yard was surrounded on either side by derelict buildings, their windows boarded, long abandoned. Empty lots that once held homes of their own were scattered about, slabs or rubble left behind. Ian took note of the loose siding and cracked paint surrounding the one he stood before and wondered who would give it to someone in his mental state.

Free was free. It was accompanied by the tram card that brought him to where he stood on the city outskirts, and the weekly grocery allowance until he found work of his own: *a new start*, they called it.

Ian's left hand held the duffle bag with what little he had to his name, and the even less he was borrowing. Phone, charger, a few items of clothing, and the last stipulation of the assistance program—a small white paper bag folded over and stapled across the top: antidepressants.

He didn't want to take them, and had made that known. Along with the belief that he wasn't truly depressed, they were a sign of all that he had lost, how far he had fallen. But he used it for a bargaining chip of his own. Ian would take the pills if he and Dr. Bardot could meet anywhere other than the hospital. He didn't tell her that the hospital dejected him further, or the shame he felt being there, but she seemed to understand. They agreed to meet in one week's time at the home office where the doctor kept her private practice.

On the front porch he turned and looked out toward the city he used to call home, watching the tram return to a place it wasn't in danger of being set on fire. Now on the outskirts, he took in the energetic city skyline, lit with the fast-paced life of hope. Hope of something gained, of something won, of love and progress. He felt the physical and emotional distance from a life he could no longer conceive, the distance between feeling a lifetime apart. It had been three days since his 'attempt' and Ian couldn't help but think of trying again, when the

1

black four-door sedan rolled to a stop.

The car door opened to an unassuming woman in her sixties, dressed in a dark skirt suit down past her knees and low-heeled shoes. A content smile was on her face as she walked slowly up the broken and faded steps of 2001 Naferty Lane. She beheld Ian, his ill-fitting clothes and three-day stubble, and held her hand out.

"You must be Ian."

He shook it, nodding, unsure what to say.

"I'm Claudia, the caretaker. What do you think?" She looked around as if proud to own this rundown black waste.

"It's very uh—nice. Thank you."

Her smile deepened and she exhaled sharply through her nose. "No need to lie. It's free, and that's what counts." She began digging in her purse when Ian spoke.

"Why?"

"Why, what?" she asked.

"Why is it free?"

"Do you want to pay?"

"I can't," he said gently to the woman. She had a grandmotherly feel that bounced between the warmth and weight of age, and a sternness that few could achieve.

"*That* is why it is free." She held out her hand once more, finally removing it from her purse. A brass key hung from a thin ring, which hung from her two pinched fingers. "I know all too well men have difficulty with the idea of charity, but you'll be needing these."

He let the remark slide and took the keys hesitantly, not wanting to argue with an elder.

Ian looked at the front door, then up at the home as a whole. "It's a bit too big for just one person."

"It feels smaller than it looks, I promise you that," she chuckled, now holding out a small white card. "In case there are any issues with the house. The hospital is less than liberal with its funds, but as caretaker I will try to accommodate necessary requests."

Ian took the card, noting the name and phone number listed.

"What if I could pay?" Ian asked, unsure why he did. He didn't have a penny to his name or a way to get one, but Claudia smiled again—at the thought or at him, he didn't know.

"Then someone else would be here."

2

The subject's name is Ian. Prone to slovenliness, substance abuse, and bouts of idleness, we have decided those who shall lead the commission, and those who shall not. Our brother, the one we must prod to action and whose spirit plagues the subject, left their quarters unlocked, in opposition to, or neglectful of, our request. The last, as always, remains in wake, as it is impossible to know the harborings of the heart. Humans have surprised us with their long-held beliefs. Ones they have locked within until the time it benefits themselves, or the time they are forced to exercise its need. We aim not to be surprised again.

Locked door after locked door, the basement, the attic, all rooms along the narrow halls of the creaky, three-story home. Claudia was right, it did feel smaller than it looked. Though tall and wide, the interior hallways were compressed and darkly lit as Ian flipped switches to flickering lights and audible electricity. A home as gloomy on the inside as it was on the outside.

Only one bedroom remained unlocked when he arrived. His other option was a foyer with a ripped Victorian-era chaise and a fireplace that looked to have been unlit since the home's inception. A dining room existed, if one could expect to eat from the dusty, well-worn table. Ian was surprised to find all eight chairs still in attendance.

In the bedroom, a mattress lay on the floor. No frame in sight but a detached and rusted metal headboard rested against the wall across from an eighties tube television sitting on a crate. Old clothes and fast food containers lay on the floor as if someone had been squatting. The bathroom had running water at least, and a mirror with only one crack.

Choosing the mattress over the chaise in the foyer, Ian searched hallway closets until he found a cover and a pillow. No sheets, not that he would have thought to put them on. To his surprise, the kitchen had a working fridge that creaked when the door opened. Few items remained on its shelves, and all oddly within their expiration dates. Whoever the last tenant was must have left recently. In a nook next to the fridge was a door, deadbolted, with an exterior padlock. Storage, perhaps.

Ian returned to his new room, rummaging through the bag with his lonely possessions and finding the debit card loaded with 70 dollars for his weekly stipend meant for food. *Hardly enough,* he'd thought. He pocketed the card and dressed in the winter clothes provided. They hung from him in wrinkled waves, at least a size too large and carrying the musty smell of hand-me-downs.

Ian left the house for the corner store he saw on the tram a quarter mile away, leaving the front door unlocked.

The bell tied to the corner store door announced Ian as he entered. He was met by a drab square room, wholly visible from the entryway. Lights buzzed overhead, casting shadows down the few and narrow aisles endcapped with cheap accessories.

"Can I help you?" asked the man behind the register.

"SKOL?" Ian asked.

The man gave a knowing look but offered the information requested, pointing to a clear handle of vodka on the bottom row of a nearby

2

shelf. The plastic caved to Ian's grip as he grabbed the container and brought it along with two others to the judgmental man at the counter. He checked out and made his way back to the house on Naferty Lane, arms hugging what would be his food for the next week.

Back in his room and still light out, Ian threw his meager duffle bag in a corner, his still uncharged phone inside. The white stapled bag stayed with him as he washed an antidepressant down with a long pull of vodka before wrapping the cover around himself. He collided with the spring mattress in hopes of relief he knew would not come.

A gray sky into a blue sky. A dark night into the dawn. Days had passed and yet Ian's haziness did not falter with the low evening light that crept through the paint-peeled shutters. Mixing alcohol and antidepressants did not seem to heighten the effect of either, but rather neutralize and reinvent. Pass time in a way he was thankful for.

Ian rolled over, looking for the relief of the vodka bottle, and instead found his charging phone. He didn't remember plugging it in, but the glowing face alerted him to the date, along with multiple missed calls and texts accumulated over the last three days. Four more until he needed to meet with the therapist. Four more that he could stay right here he was.

He opened the phone. Calls and texts repeated from the same three people, growing increasingly frantic. He skipped over the voicemails, reading only the texts.

Where are you?

Are you okay?

Your neighbors said they saw an ambulance leaving your place. We called the hospital but they wouldn't tell us what happened. Please call us.

He had never told them, his parents and his brother, just how bad things had become. The thought of even having that conversation drained whatever energy he had, and Ian dropped the phone, replacing it with a nearby vodka bottle.

Empty. He reached for another. Empty. Pushing over the third bottle barely within his grasp, he felt the featherlight pull of the depleted jug. Ian looked around through squinted eyes in disbelief. A headache from hell and not having the energy for the long winter walk, he curled into a ball under the cover and begged for relief, as he had for an entire year. It had not come then. He did not know why he thought it would now.

For three months he had begged for it to go away. Begged to a god he didn't believe in. Screamed and shouted and cried until he fell asleep late into the night. Tried everything he could think of until he was out of ideas and only one remained. Now he lay in an empty house, hatred and betrayal, hope and happiness all lost to him. It would start with the numbness of grief. Overwhelmed with the pit he resided in until the emotion broke through, little difference between crying and pleading as the cycle began again.

Ian muttered into the night, as he had all that time, "Make it go away, make it go away. Just make it go away."

This time, before the darkness of the dusk took him, he swore it spoke back.

"Rest," it said.

3

Ian didn't feel the absence of it.

It was replaced, momentarily, with a woman. She wasn't doing anything. They were not doing anything, just being. Words were said, Ian not able to make them out, surrounded by a sunny day with no edges. An incomplete vision, focused on her, all in white and under a tree, limbs stretched into the faded corners while she lay in his lap. The light of her eyes and the glow of her smile, familiar and comfortable, until she was gone.

And with her, the relief of the unconscious. Ian woke in the daylight, feeling the grief settle back into his body, compressing his entire being.

For the first time in over a year, he felt a moment of relief, and witnessed as it fled him. He almost wished it had not happened, had not given him something more that could be taken away. So small, yet more than he thought possible. A dream as thick and real as the cold of the winter morning he only now noticed.

His breath shot out before him as he wrapped the blanket around himself and rolled to his stomach, pushing to his knees. Through the broken shutters he could see the thick powder of a winter snow. The morning sun cast a house-shaped shadow on the street, narrow tread marks through the otherwise perfect layer of pure white.

Ian wondered if the heating was broken or had never been turned on. It had been cold these past few days, increasingly, he remembered through the haze of the hangover. The bright leaves, whether on the ground or clinging to branches outside his hospital room had turned a dull brown, mixed and mashed with the earth outside his window. The house had been tepid when he arrived. Tepid, but not frozen.

Broken.

He rolled from bed, not bothering to fish his thicker clothes from the bag, instead opting to take the cover with him on his search for a thermostat. His bare feet were hardly noticeable against the cold wood floors over the pounding of his head.

Ian found a thermostat no newer than 1980 in the living room. He knew little about devices from that time, but couldn't see an indication of power, or if it used it. He noted the red line on 68 degrees, and moved the needle back and forth. Nothing happened. Another thought occurred.

He made his way to the kitchen and opened the fridge. No light.

It wasn't just the thermostat. The house had lost power.

Ian found a window and noted the closest inhabited house, a full block over, had lights on in an upstairs window. It was possible the power cutoff was between the streets, though Ian knew it was not likely. He re-explored the first and second floors of the home before a sinking feeling crept into his gut. The breaker box would be in the basement, behind the padlocked door.

He made his way to the kitchen and tried the handle, disregarding the thick padlock and confirming what he already knew before picking up his phone.

It rang three times before Claudia answered.

"Ian. How are you?" she asked concisely.

"Miss—" Ian started, not realizing in time that he did not know the homeowner's last name. He skipped over it. "I think the storm tripped a breaker. Is the box in the basement?"

"Oh, yes," she said. Ian was quiet for a moment, thinking she'd add

3

more. She did not.

"It's locked," he said, staring at the door as if it would open at the acknowledgment.

"Liability reasons. I'm sure you understand. Dark and damp down there. Don't need anyone getting hurt."

"I—yes. But I need access to it," Ian said, flustered as he became more aware of his extremities, and the lack of solutions being presented for this unfamiliar home.

"No need. I will send someone tomorrow. Doubtful I can get them on a weekend."

"Miss…" he started again in a plea, "Claudia, it must be 40 degrees in—"

"There's a fireplace in the foyer. I would suggest making use of it," she said. Ian tried to interject a question but was cut off again. "I must go now, but try to stay warm."

She hung up the phone before Ian could respond, his anger momentarily heating him enough to forget the cold. He leaned his head against the locked door, a knock sounding when his forehead hit the wood. He slowly breathed in and out one time, calming his frustration before he thought he heard a single faint knock echo back.

Drunk. That's how he would do this. If he had to find wood and start a fire, he might as well be drunk. He probably still was, with the things he was hearing.

Fully clothed in the only thick winter set provided, Ian headed down the snow-covered quarter-mile to restock on supplies, only to find a small rectangular sign hung from inside the door.

Closed.

It was Sunday, he realized. No liquor sales.

Too tired and hungover to be angry, Ian went back to the house. He climbed the rickety, faded stairs, opened the door he had not bothered to lock, and went inside. Little difference in the temperature from the outside, Ian sat down on a kitchen stool and hung his head in his hands.

This is my life.

How many moments had he found himself at a cross with decision fatigue and hopelessness? The desires of the day taken from him, one step at a time. The small light of this morning, that woman's face, the dream—as gone as the heat and the alcohol.

Head still in hand, Ian felt a shift in the room. The feeling of presence. Not of being watched, but of space being filled. He lifted his head, his heart beating an extra time and noticed there, on the opposite end of the kitchen counter, his pills. The antidepressants.

Ian stood, moving to the bottle and clasping them in one hand, trying to recall the actions of the muddled morning. He remembered the woman. The bitter cold. The white of the desolate street. Rambling around the home, the thermostat and the locked door and the sound he imagined. His cell phone had been in one hand, the other holding the cover tightly around him, but he did not remember taking the bottle from the room.

He poured the contents out before him and began counting. He was given thirty days' worth and remembered taking one, nearly a week ago on the first night. Everything after that was a blur.

Twenty-seven…twenty-eight…twenty-nine.

He had only taken the one. Mixed with vodka and more vodka, he had neglected this crucial part of his deal with Dr. Bardot, who he was to meet with in the morning. Unable to be kicked out so soon and without a plan, Ian searched the kitchen cabinets.

Plates, pots, pans, many shining and noticeably newer than their surroundings. At last he found the glassware, pulling out the cleanest one he could find. There would be no warm water but Ian gave a sigh of relief that the pipes had not frozen over in the night, before downing one of the blue and white capsules.

Claudia suggested a fire. The question he was to ask, which he did not get to before the call's abrupt ending—*With what wood?*

None was located in the foyer, next to the fireplace that appeared not to have been used since the home's inception, nor did he see any stacked around the home when he arrived. Ian made his way outside, finding twigs and small tree branches that had snapped in the frigid air. Not enough for a full day or a roaring fire, but he had a plan for the larger pieces.

Kindling located, Ian took the remaining money unspent on alcohol and headed to the tram station. He would get more tomorrow at the one-week mark, which he could use to replenish the vodka when sales reopened. He had asked Dr. Bardot why deposits were weekly, instead of biweekly or monthly. She simply said, "So it can't be spent all at once." As if that would stop him from spending it the way he chose.

The tram brought him to a neighborhood market. Cold cuts, liquid butane, a few small candlesticks, and a longneck lighter were all he could afford, and all he felt competent to make use of.

The sun was going down behind the western patched roofs as he arrived back at Naferty Lane. He lit the candles and placed them between the kitchen, his room and the foyer, illuminating what little he could of the decrepit space. He dragged his mattress and blanket through the halls, setting it before the fireplace, before grabbing one of the dining room chairs from the table in the other room.

An antique that matched the table. It could be as old as the home was. Nineteenth century at the earliest, with beautiful upholstery and solid wood. Intricate carvings along the back and arms. It was the most ragged of the bunch, but priceless nonetheless. Ian lifted it over his head and smashed it on the floor.

Two hind legs broke, splintering off in separate directions. He lifted it again, throwing it down with full force, separating the back and bottom of the chair. He broke off the remaining two legs from the seat and gathered the spread-out pieces next to the hearth.

Ian soaked twigs in butane a few minutes before igniting them, then added larger pieces on top. When the small fire was good and steady, Ian added more sticks and pieces of the chair, and noticed the smoke was not exiting the chimney. He hoped the flue was closed, rather than the fireplace being clogged. In this old home, an animal carcass could be stuck inside, or birds could have built nests at the top.

He crouched to his knees, searching for a handle to the flue, trying to relieve the smoke. Fumbling about, his eyes burned as his hands scraped across brick and stone, exploring and not finding. The larger pieces began to catch fire, smoke billowing out faster into Ian's face and filling the foyer.

"Left," came a faint voice.

Ian jumped, twisting to look in every corner of the room. Squinting through the throb in his eyes. He saw no legs, no body. He heard nothing prior to this. Not footsteps or a door opening. It was not the first sound he had imagined in this home. Ian turned reluctantly to the fire, not wanting to put his back to the open room but feeling the need to focus on the smoke. The flames were too tall now; he couldn't peek his head inside to look up at the flue. An ancient fireplace toolset lay to the left of the hearth. He grabbed the iron poker, barbed at the end, shoving up into the flue and hitting metal. *Closed.*

The smoke was a flurry, coming out lower the thicker it became. Ian closed his eyes for relief and held his breath in the close distance of the flame and smoke as he tried using the pointed end to find an opening and pry. He hit brick and metal, brick and metal, unable to distinguish what he searched for. Unsuccessful after a moment, he pulled his head away, opening his eyes.

In the smoke, he saw a face.

Not a face. A skull. Not a human skull; too angular. Too jagged. It sloped up to an unbroken crown of bone. A thin mouth and hollow eyes attached to a lithe frame, as rigid as the head it bore.

Ian lurched backward, moving with his hands and legs but not letting go of the iron poker. He watched, horrified and heart thrumming, as the crowned beast's human-like body moved in the shadows of the smoke.

It did not come toward him.

Turning its back to Ian, it leaned left, reaching out to the side of the hearth and the remaining ancient fireplace tools. Ian blinked rapidly at his burning eyes and the sound of metal scraping metal. He alternated eyes to try to keep one open at all times on this otherworldly being. He tightened his grip on the iron poker, backing away further until his head battered the lipped alcove of a window seal. Ian winced, closing both eyes briefly at the pain, holding the iron poker up to his shoulder ready to swing.

When he opened them again, the creature was gone.

Before he knew it, it was freezing once again. Rays of early-morning sunshine peeked through the cracks in the slatted window shades. He had fallen asleep, he realized, against the wall waiting out the creature he thought he saw. Not risking pulling the mattress from the center of the room over to his corner, he had slept on the wooden floor. But as he looked to the ash-filled fireplace, he found his fear had gone with the night.

The smoke was gone now. The room felt empty; the entire house did, as he took in his surroundings of broken chair parts and spilled wax candles. Ian remembered looking from one side of the room to the other, over and over trying to catch another glimpse, until late into the night when the darkness fell heavy on his eyes.

He remembered, as clear as the room before him now, the crowned figure in the smoke. The gangly body of ridges and points. The hollow eyes.

Didn't he?

In the bright chill of the morning, he felt it impossible now. Things like that did not exist. Nightmares and hallucinations were not real, and that was what it must have been. After all, he was unharmed and untouched. An entire night unprotected and without incident. Monsters do not leave their prey untouched. But he had never seen something like that before. *Not before the medications,* he thought.

That's when all of this started. The dreams he was having, the voice he heard, the Being he saw. It all began that first night, when he took the first antidepressant. Ian knew he had never been prone to seeing or hearing things that were not there. Regardless of his mental state, he knew he was not crazy. The only thing that could have pushed him over the edge was a chemical change, an outside force. He would have to do something about that. For now, he had to get warm.

Rubbing his eyes, still burning from smoke and poor sleep, he thought of the day. Today was important. *Wasn't it?* But he had no responsibilities, he thought, as he got up to find more clothes, more kindling, and his phone to check the time.

He was correct, as he roamed the house; it was as empty and cold as it felt. Not just in temperature, but in invitation. Somehow the degradation of the property stood out more today than on others. It had a strange feel to it. Locked doors, peeling paint, creaky floors, and old furniture. Hollow in every way except...presence.

The kitchen counters were unencumbered by anything but the scattered pills he'd counted the previous morning. Ian walked to them, picked up the bottle and peeled the folded label to read the side effects, though there was only one he was looking for. And he found it, alongside a number of other physical ailments. He figured he should be happy for the one he had.

...Nausea, diarrhea, skin lesions, joint and muscle pain, decreased alertness...

3

"Fuck," he breathed out, realizing what he was forgetting. The meeting with *Dr. Bardot*. She would expect him to be taking the pills, but he couldn't. He knew he couldn't take them anymore with his new hallucinations.

Ian looked up from the counter. As he set eyes on the locked basement door, he saw the second thing he had forgotten. *The repair man.*

Ian found his phone and called Claudia while changing. He found her instruction odd: "Just leave the home unlocked. They'll figure out the rest."

He pressed, insisting that wasn't wise, and anyhow, how would they get into the basement? But Claudia just said with a cheer in her voice, "What would they even take?"

He stuffed what few possessions he'd be leaving behind under the bathroom counter, pills included, and glanced in bewilderment one last time at the locked basement door before heading out.

4

"You're still not sleeping."

Dr. Bardot's home office was quaint. Distinctly unlike the decoration of her office at the hospital. Where beige and white would have been were patterns and color. Not bright or outlandish, but neutral and inviting. Cozy and well put together, like a place well lived in. He wondered what the rest of her home must look like.

Having accessed this office through the side gate of her suburban property, Ian had only seen the small wilted garden that lined the home's exterior on his way in. A tram ride, a public bus, and a long walk to get there, but still better than the hospital, he thought.

"No foreplay then?" he asked.

She didn't respond.

"Did you expect that to change?" Ian continued.

Dr. Bardot had cut straight to the chase upon his arrival, though he had to admit his relief at not being asked the dreaded question *How are you?* Everyone always asked it, though no one wanted a real answer.

"I had hoped so, with the medication and a roof over your head. How is the new home?" she asked, already scribbling notes.

'It's a place to sleep.'

"And the medication. You're taking it?"

"Mhm."

She put down the pen and they sat in silence for a moment, Dr.

4

Bardot not taking notes or probing further, but just staring at him, waiting.

"I thought we had an agreement, Ian. I'd tell you what I think, if you truly do the same."

"What do you want to know?" he asked, fake earnestness on his lips.

"Expound, Ian. Don't force me to play twenty-one questions. Offer information without being prodded for it," she said. "I can't help you if you insist on this charade; if you refuse to help yourself."

Ian sucked in a breath, too tired to argue, and said the first thing that came to his mind, tumbling all together. "The house is a shithole."

Bardot stared at him further, waiting again.

He took another deep breath. "Hasn't been kept up in years. Shutters are practically falling off the hinges, paint peeling on every wall. First week and the A/C is already broken. It's 12 degrees outside. It's being fixed now, I hope, but half the rooms are locked. Feels like a rundown mental ward."

"And information about you?" she asked, breezing over his complaints. He found an odd sense of comfort in his ability to rant without repercussion.

"No, I am not sleeping," Ian answered her previous question, rubbing the bridge of his nose.

"What occupies your mind when you lie down?" she asked, pen back in hand and scribbling furiously.

That was not something he intended to share. However, it would do no harm to tell her what he was experiencing. What he had seen last night. It wasn't any worse than thoughts of suicide, or actually trying to kill himself. If they locked him in a mental ward it would probably come with better accommodations than his current situation.

"I think the pills are making—"

Don't.

Ian froze. That voice. There it was again. The one he heard last night.

25

The one in the fire. He looked around the room, but saw nothing out of place.

Bardot followed his eye movements. "You think what?" she asked.

She must not have heard the sound. So it was in his head, he thought, partially relieved and partially solemn.

"I think—"

Do not tell her that.

He froze again, his eyes widening at the clipped tone he heard closer than possible. She hadn't heard it that time either, her face pulled into a wince of concern. Perhaps he wouldn't tell her. Not to listen to the voice, but because he heard the voice as clear as if someone was sitting next to him. Clearer, as if it were his own thoughts echoing in his mind. Whatever he was experiencing, it was more vivid than a mere hallucination.

"Sorry," Ian said. "I believe the medication is...changing the way I think."

Dr. Bardot hesitated but wrote a note that time.

Where did the voice go? So distinct just moments before, and now—silence.

"Do I have to take them?" Ian asked. "They seem to be making things worse."

The doctor finished her scribbles and looked up. "It can often seem that way while we are healing. I assure you, you are better off with them. The home may be—undesirable, but I do not control the housing program. The medication remains a stipulation of your enrollment," she said with finality.

"They make me feel numb."

"Are you sure that's not the alcohol?" she asked.

Did he smell like alcohol? He hadn't drunk since Saturday. His face must have given away his thoughts, as she said, "67 degrees in here and a fraction of that outside, and yet you're sweating. Can't sit still.

4

Shaking hands—"

"It helps."

"Every alcoholic claims that, until they can't anymore."

"I *am not* an alcoholic," Ian snapped with impatience.

Bardot scribbled on her pad again. "Why did that evoke an emotional response?"

Ian had his beliefs about alcoholism, having lost his share of friends to the bottle. They had all claimed the same thing. *If I start, I can't stop.*

"I didn't drink to excess for thirty-two years, and alcoholism didn't infect me like a cold in the night. I can stop. I *choose* not to. You shouldn't just throw that label around; it diminishes the hard reality for the people who truly have it."

"I apologize," she said, changing the subject. "Have you started the job search?"

He could tell she wasn't fully bought in, but regressed nonetheless. Probably out of good sense in choosing her battles rather than being in agreement.

"Not quite."

"It can take time to place in a good position. I would suggest starting sooner rather than later to ensure proper runway," she said, taking more notes.

Six months. That's how long he had the house for through the program. After that, who knew.

"Do you have any prospects? Anywhere to begin looking?" she asked.

Ian sat there, unable to answer. Who would he call that would pick up? Even if they did, no one would put their name on the line to help him get a job after what he had done.

"You used to work in finance, if I'm not mistaken."

She wasn't mistaken. She wouldn't be, on anything that was in that file of his. He still wondered what it told of his former life.

"They revoked my licenses," Ian said to answer this line of question-

27

ing. Series 6. Series 7. Series 63. They took them all. "I can't so much as open a spreadsheet in a firm now."

"Surely there are skills you learned there that would still be of use. Hard skills that could transfer into a less...regulated role."

When he didn't respond, she suggested it could be "Something to think about," but he had already thought through it all. He didn't want anything to do with that former life. Anything that reminded him of what he'd had and since lost. The hours, days, weeks, months, and years spent building a life that had slipped through his fingers despite how tightly he held it.

"We have a few more things to get to before you can go," she said. "Have you had any more thoughts of suicide?"

Ian met her gaze and answered honestly. "Yes."

"Do you intend to act on them?" she asked in earnest.

"No."

"Why not?"

Many would have heard this as a challenge, as a beckoning to violence. Ian however, knew what she meant. He knew it by the look on her face of true empathy and wonder. It wasn't pity, but a desire to know just how much he meant it.

Why wouldn't he this time, if he did last time?

"I'm not sure. The inspiration is yet to strike."

She took in a deep breath, further breaking the stoic composure she should be keeping. "That doesn't inspire confidence, Ian."

"Do I look like I'm swimming in confidence?" he asked.

She ignored the barb. "If anything changes, will you reach out?"

"Yes," he said again, less truthfully this time. "Are we done here?"

"Very well," she conceded. "That's progress, I suppose. There's one last order of business while you're here."

Bardot stood up and went to her desk, pulled open a drawer he could not see, and palmed a mid-sized clear plastic container in one hand and a white medically sealed lid in the other. She walked over and handed them to him, before looking over her shoulder to the open bathroom door.

He would pass this drug test, he knew. But with the voices he heard and the things he saw—how much longer would it matter?

☦

Ian was being stared at.

His neck prickled with the attention of a focused gaze. The tram car was full of commuters; daily passengers to and from work, school, and the like. People attentive to their own lives, except for one. Ian turned and met the stare of a man around his age. Not a casual meeting of the eyes; a brief glance of curiosity. No, this man was staring at Ian like he knew him.

He wouldn't have thought too much of it, normally. Public transportation seemed to carry all those who wouldn't be seen in daylight. But this man was different. He was in a suit, far too nice for a tram, Ian thought. If he could afford that suit, those oxfords, and that haircut, he could afford his own car. Dark hair and dusky skin in agreeable contrast, not a hair out of place or a scuff on his shoes. *Maybe he's like me.* It was conceivable the man could have lost his license. It wasn't unheard of to be rich with a penchant for drinking and driving. But that was not what stood out about him the most.

Ian had seen him earlier, at the bus stop heading to Dr. Bardot's home. The man climbed onto that bus, stayed through six stops, and got off when Ian did. Ian allowed himself to shake off the coincidence as the man got to his feet before Ian when leaving the bus. But now he rode the same tram line as well, and they were almost to his stop.

Five seats over and catty corner to Ian, the stare continued, deadpan. Ian looked away, out toward the neighborhoods they passed, shifting in his seat before peeking again. The man's eyes stayed locked on him.

"Can I help you?" Ian asked.

A smirk moved up the side of the stranger's face. Breathing a short laugh out through the nose, he turned away.

Unnerved, Ian wrapped his arms around himself. Others were on the tram, though he felt vulnerable. Public transportation horror stories flooded his mind, realizing he had no means of protection should this stranger attempt to rob or attack him.

As the man looked away, so did Ian. He peeked back occasionally but the man had moved on, now on the phone and talking to someone in a low, inaudible voice, acting as if he didn't know Ian existed. To his relief, when the tram stopped next and Ian stood up, the stranger remained seated.

The walk back to Naferty Lane was neither long enough nor cold enough to pull his mind from the dejected feeling. Questions coursed through him not in words but in unfettered emotions, flowing from one to the next. Anger, confusion, surprise, and guilt. Ian wondered if the man was from his past, but did not remember him. He thought he would remember someone as good looking as that.

The thoughts were shaken loose as he approached the house. There was mail on the stoop. Two envelopes, addressed to him. One from *Westerton Memorial Hospital*. The other from *Savor Emergency Services*. His heart sank to his stomach as he opened them, the anxiety mounting. It was as he feared. Tens of thousands of dollars for his involuntary hospital stay, another handful for the ambulance he didn't call. That he couldn't even remember being in.

Defeat rattled him as he approached the door and pulled out his keys, before remembering he never locked it. Ian turned back to the street. The only noticed change was the black Lincoln SUV parked caddy corner to the property. Not exactly Ian's idea of a blue-collar vehicle; He hoped he was getting back after the repair man, and not before.

Ian reached out and turned the handle, opening it to a wave that warmed his face and slightly stung his eyes.

4

Thank God.

Locking the door behind him and shedding his coat, he made his way to the kitchen and stopped dead in his tracks at the sight of the repair man hunched over, peering into his refrigerator.

It took too long for Ian to notice the man's clothes did not match that thought.

He was wearing a suit, with perfectly coiffed hair. Standing up and turning around, the stranger said, "You should not have told her those things."

5

His coat slipped from his hand, the bills following. Ian was having difficulty thinking clearly over the pounding in his ears as his heart accelerated rapidly. He froze, staring at the man, who stared back, silence echoing between them. The stranger's face was unreadably neutral to Ian's own worried expression.

"I told you not to," he said.

"Who are you?" Ian managed to croak.

"You do not recognize me?" Cold. Unemotional.

Ian tried to think beyond the events of the day, to search for meaning, understanding; the shock not allowing him to drift further than the last few hours and the immediate danger in front of him.

"The bus. You were on the—"

"Before then," the stranger said, cutting him off.

Ian's heart sank further into his stomach. Of course. *A client.*

He had blocked so much of the last year from his mind. Unraveling at losing his wife, he had paid little attention to his work, to his clients, many of whom lost substantial amounts as he paid less and less attention to their portfolios. To try and recuperate the losses, he had switched from moderate-risk investments to heavy risk with higher return rates. A perfectly legal, though unethical, way of managing financial assets—and one that lost him his licenses and his career. He was not legally responsible for those losses, but he had not left them behind with his old life.

"I'm sorry. I can get it back," Ian said.

"You cannot take back something said. Once it is spoken, it no longer belongs to you."

What does that mean?

The man moved slowly around the counter, never taking his eyes off Ian and closing half the distance between them.

Ian took a step back, opening his mouth and raising his hands in defense before his plea was cut off by a different voice.

"You talkin' in riddles again?" A short brown-haired man, the opposite to the taller one in every discernible way, moved in from the direction of Ian's bedroom. His head was buzzed and a shaped beard of scruff outlined his jaw. He had a good face but it was hardly noticeable given the outlandish tracksuit he wore. Ian's hands remained raised as he took another step back from his prior client and the companion. The shorter one barely paid attention to him and walked to the thermostat.

"You mind? Rather hot in here," he said in a muddled Irish accent.

Ian didn't respond as the man proceeded with his back to them. The taller one still stared, unwavering.

"Introduce yourself yet?" the short man asked, turning.

"No. Waiting on—"

The floorboards creaked above their heads, the sound of footsteps lightly carrying. There was another one in the house. Upstairs.

"I know who you are," Ian blurted. "I can fix this." He didn't know who they were, though. At least not by name. Ian had rarely met his past clients, mostly brought on by referrals. He had no idea what they'd lost at his hands.

"I think if you were capable of fixin' it, you wouldn't have tried to fuck a toaster in the bath," the short one said.

He'd make it slow, draw it out, Ian thought. There would be no pleading. His eyes darted to the door, there was nothing blocking the way. It was locked now but he could probably get there and turn the handle before—

The clacking of heels on wood sounded from the stairwell. The room grew silent as the footsteps approached, going from the hollow steps of stairs to the finality of the ground floor with a solid thud.

A woman walked out, breathtakingly beautiful. She was between the two others in height with black hair and black clothing, understated and complex. Clinging to her in waves. Ian thought he saw a light in her eyes as she found her place beside them, but when their eyes met, she turned hers down, staring at the floor. Ian felt a small tinge of relief; she wasn't nearly as imposing as the others.

"Ian," the tall man said, pulling Ian's attention back to him. He swore the man hadn't blinked since they began talking. "We have things to discuss."

"I know, just tell me how much you—" Ian started but the shorter one cut him off again with a laugh.

"If he's already talkin' about money, he won't need much time with Gio."

The tall one narrowed his gaze, hands moving to rest in his pockets. "Who do you think we are?" he asked.

Ian swallowed. "Clients."

"No," was all the man said, before his face hollowed out.

His eyes grew dark, the edges of his sockets fading like a black hole, the skin itself becoming pallid. The top of his head grew rigid, his hair replaced by a crown of bone. The body did not change, only the face. The face of the beast Ian had seen in the smoke. His mouth moved with no lips, showing every pointed tooth and taut muscle of his jaw as a familiar voice reverberated through the room.

"We met last night."

5

⸸

Ian scrambled back further, into a wall. *Impossible.* He was seeing things, he was sure of it now. He should have told the therapist of his hallucinations, of the voices he was hearing. He closed his eyes, squeezing them shut, counting breaths and willing them away. This wasn't real. It was twelve months of pain and suffering. It was loss and grief. It was his subconscious, forcing his hand to try again.

But when he opened his eyes, they were still there.

The man's face had returned to the perfect dusk skin and marbled hair. None of the three moved from where they stood, allowing Ian to press his back to the corner he had found in the kitchen walls. They looked at him, unafraid and unfaltering, save for the short one, bemusement dancing on his face.

"My favorite part, this is," he said. "I'd show you mine, but you might piss yourself on me floors."

The woman nudged him in what looked like a desire for him to stop talking.

"You're just hallucinations. You're not real." Ian said it out loud. He said it to himself.

The tall one reached out lazily and swiped a glass off the counter. It shattered with a dull ripple, sending shards of glass out around their feet. The man adjusted his feet slightly, crunching bits beneath his soles.

"Who did that, then?"

I did, I must've. It's all in my head. It's all in my head. It's all in my head.

The man moved closer to him now, the other two following suit.

Ian wanted to run. To scream. To do anything. His body froze between doubt and fear. Panic seized him as they neared, eyes shooting between the three vastly different people who stood there.

The woman broke the silence. "We are not here to hurt you," she said.

He almost wanted to believe the gentle caress in her tone.

"Why are you here then?" he asked.

"To help."

"With *what?*" His voice broke, still cowering in the corner, but his eyes met hers. He did not want help. He wanted them to leave. He wanted his mind back. He wanted this house that was not a home. He wanted peace.

"Ian," the husky voice of the tall man cut through. Calm.

He didn't take his eyes off the woman, pleading for it to end.

"Ian." A sharp rasp.

He reluctantly looked, meeting the eyes that were hollow just moments ago.

"We are the Spirits of Cardinal Rapture. You are in our home—and we are at your service."

That was the last thing Ian heard before he fainted.

⸸

Hands were on him. He was on a couch. A couch he had seen before, faded red and velvet. No, a chaise, the one in the foyer.

Ian blinked away the fog of his thoughts, looking around the dimly lit space, and saw them. Just as they were, three faces of serenity, and sorrow, and indifference.

"Are you with us?" the woman asked.

Ian didn't know what to say, so he just nodded, not meeting their eyes. The tall one had said something just before Ian had passed out. This was their home. They lived here, and Ian was a guest. They called themselves something—something Ian refused to believe. But he also knew he had seen and heard things he could not explain. The presence he felt in the house, the pills appearing in the kitchen, his phone charging itself. It was either all a hallucination and lost memories, or none of it was.

"Prove it."

5

It was all he could think to say. These three in front of him claimed to be spirits. Spirits of Cardinal Rapture. One of them presented a face Ian knew was not possible; the other two still seemed as human as he was himself.

He had two options in front of him.

He could accept he was losing his mind—that the medications and the alcohol were causing him to see things and hear things he could not explain; that they caused him to do things he could not remember.

Or, he could have them prove their existence. He felt a fool for even considering it an option, but it was better than the alternative, he supposed.

"Prove it," Ian said again.

"Prove what?" the short man asked, hands raised to his sides. He looked to be enjoying the scene far less than he had in the kitchen.

"Prove you are who you say you are."

"Ian…"

"You're claiming you're not human. Do something a…non-human could do."

The tall man started. "Did I not just—"

"For all I know, you and your skull face are a figment of my imagination. Show me something else. One of the others," he looked at the woman and shorter man. "You do something."

"Our essence is not a party trick for your amusement."

"I am anything but amused," Ian shot back. He had lived there a full week, vacant silence his only companion. Bombarded with claims of the supernatural, he could not deny what he had seen, nor would he welcome it with ease.

The two looked at each other, a non-verbal drawing of straws that settled on the woman. A reluctant look on her face, but one she was resigned to before the decision was even made, apparent that they did not want the mouthy man to take up the task.

She did not say anything—none of them did—as she walked up and grabbed Ian's sweat-slicked hand with her own. But this gesture was not her answer to his test, Ian realized; it was only to steady him as she reached up with her other hand and placed it on his cheek.

He tried to pull back, not quickly enough. The second it connected, he was no longer in the kitchen with these three strange people. He did not remember the kitchen, had never been there before. This was his life. In this park, on this sunny summer day, with his wife and two little girls.

His wife. They were married. What was her name? He didn't need to know it, he loved her regardless. He loved the life they lived, that they had built. He had seen her before. Where? It did not matter. The past did not matter. He was here with her now. With them. They were everything. They were happiness, they were peace, and they were not his.

Nausea and reality washed over Ian. The weight of his body was heavy on the soles of his feet, the atmosphere returning to the dry and hollow kitchen. Skin was touching his, unfamiliar and timid. Not his wife's, not the woman he loved so deeply and yet too briefly. It pulled away, the pale arm returning to the woman looking up at him with the beaded knowing eyes of sorrow.

Ian did not scramble back or push her away. He stood there, frozen and incredulous at the waking dream he had returned from. Her hand was removed from his cheek but the one on his own still remained, only removed when she saw the look of horror on his face as he locked eyes with her.

"What are you?" he croaked.

She gave a soft smile with a tilted head, a failed attempt to relieve the pain etched across his face.

"Desire," she said.

Desire. She was claiming to be the Spirit of Desire, and he found himself believing her. She had shown him something he hadn't even known he wanted. Ian would have stayed there all day and into the night if the tall man had not spoken first, drawing the attention of all three to himself.

"Will that suffice?"

Ian could not answer. He was still in that dream. In that park. *He had kids.* What he would give to return to them.

☦

"One more time. You're the—"

They had shifted positions. Ian remained on the couch, opposite to the end where the woman sat, her beauty radiating in the dimly lit room. The hollowness she had left him with after her touch had not dissipated. *Desire*, she called herself.

The taller man stood by the hearth, idly swirling the ashes left behind. The shorter one paced the length of the room, fidgety in his own right. Though he was slowly calming to their presence, Ian still found himself on edge as they answered his rapid-fire questions in a way indicating this was not their first time doing so.

"The Spirits of Cardinal Rapture."

"And what exactly does that mean?"

"We are vassals of the Cardinal Angels—the original embodiments of essence we now carry," the tall man said.

"We're glorified servants," cut in the woman, the man glowering back. "We embody the spirits of inclinations that…unburden the soul."

"Can you speak like people?" Ian asked them.

It was the short man dressed in the plaid tracksuit who answered. "We're the fun ones, mate. Some weep and drag and whine about everythin' under the stars. We're the ones they want to be."

Ian looked between them, noticing again their vast differences.

"You are each a different one, then. A different spirit?" he asked, and the woman who called herself Desire nodded.

That hollow feeling in his chest rose again before her eyes cut to the shorter man, who dropped his to the floor, his lips in a tight line.

"Who's who?"

"Dignity," said the tall man, who too looked at the shorter one.

"Passion," he said with a smile that did not meet his eyes.

"Dignity, Desire and Passion. And you—" A cough.

Ian met the gaze of the tall one, the one called Dignity. He looked it as well. In fact, Ian thought, Desire did too. They both carried themselves with an air that projected the spirit they embodied. Dignity was attractive, but not unbearably so. Everything was pressed and clean, his movements fluid and speech unfaltering. His gait and posture resolute with intention.

Desire, for her part, was exactly that. Men and women alike would kill to be with her. She looked like no one he had ever seen, dressed like no one he had ever known. More than that, he felt it in her presence. He felt the pull of want, though it echoed in an empty chamber of his heart. He craved to be back in the embrace of her vision. To live in the dream she had fabricated. Ian could not tell if it felt more real than where he stood, or if he only wanted it to.

Passion, though, was not what Ian would have pictured of the man. He had a sleaziness to him that put Ian on edge.

"There are others," Dignity said.

"Other what?"

"Spirits."

"Where?" Ian looked around as if they would appear before him like Dignity in the smoke, all gray skin and unnatural features.

"Not here, at the moment," Dignity replied.

Ian's heart returned to his stomach, the eminent feeling of danger coming back. The locked rooms and their unknown contents. Strangers. These were just strangers to him, ones who claimed to be celestial beings of some kind. He found his belief pulled back, crowded

5

with the fear of the unknown.

"How many?" he asked.

Passion held up a hand and started fake counting on his fingers, miming numbers to himself. Once again, the three exchanged glances, saying with their eyes what they could not, or did not want to, with their mouths.

"Seven," Dignity answered after a moment, as Passion counted on his second hand.

Ian started. "Wait."

Spirits of inclinations that unburden the soul. The fun ones. Dignity, Desire, Passion—seven.

They realized it the same moment Ian did. The other two shifted, Dignity's move barely perceptible but it was there. Desire's face pulled tight, and a wide grin grew on Passion's, who had stopped pacing, humor and delight returning to his features.

"You're the fucking seven deadly sins."

6

"I have always hated that name," said the Spirit of Dignity. "It reeks of ignorance."

"What would you prefer to be called?" mocked Ian, rising from where he sat, eyes burning from where he had buried them in his palms.

"There are many names your people have given us in history. The Nafs, the Poisons, the Thieves—"

"Only thing I've ever stolen was a woman's heart. Hardly a sin," cut in the Spirit of Passion.

Dignity eyed him scornfully. He must be the leader. "You may call us what you wish. I simply made a statement," Dignity finished.

"Let's say, extremely theoretically, that I believe you are spirits. *Demons*," he spit the word, viewing these in particular to be the opposite of Angels, "why would the seven deadly sins want to *help* me?"

"It is our directive."

"*Speak. Like. A. Person.*"

"It is recompense," said Desire, "our sentencing for past transgressions. To help humans better their lives, until our quota is fulfilled."

"That's what's supposed to convince me? That I'm next up on the depth chart to get you out of prison? You can't be serious."

"There are many rules," said Dignity placatingly. "We cannot lie to, or kill, or maim humans, for starters."

"*You just lied about who you are,*" Ian said.

6

"Words are capricious. As long as they mean what you mean when you say them, technically you told the truth," said Passion, moving to take Ian's now unoccupied seat.

Ian took a deep breath to steady himself. To stop from lashing out or laughing in puzzlement, he did not know which.

"This isn't real. You're not real," Ian said.

"Are we back to this already?"

"You just told me the seven deadly sins are serving a prison sentence and I'm their way out. You expect me to believe this?"

"Spirits *of* the deadly sins, and should you not?" asked Dignity. "Our sins are against humanity, so must be our restitution. If we fail, we continue, stuck in our damnation. If we succeed, you are better off for it."

And if they failed, he would be right back where he started.

"You can have as many names as you like, I'm still not buying this story, so why don't you get the fuck out of my—" Ian stopped himself. Such a small thing and yet he could not say it. *My house.* This was not his house. He did not want it to be. It couldn't be.

Dignity smiled, his first since the tram that morning. "That is right, Ian. You do not have a home. You do not have a family. You are unemployed, and..." he looked Ian up and down. At his clothes and hair and body. The Spirit's face grew more serious. "...Undesirable."

Ian, for all the hatred and contempt he felt at this trespassing man he had only just met, could not force himself to fight back. To prove him wrong. He wasn't wrong. It was true, and he knew it. His wife had left him, he did not have kids, he had lost his job, and had stopped taking care of himself long before the former.

"What do you want?" Ian asked, contempt still hot on his tongue.

"We come here offering aid and you dare to ask us what *we* want?"

Ian breathed in deeply, unable to tell if he was growing tired of this charade, or leaning into it. "Aid with what?" he asked.

The shorter brown-haired man chuckled. "You're broke, love. In the worst shape of your life, I hope, and moanin' in the night about some lady who ain't here." The man looked around the room, mock searching.

Desire shifted her weight on the couch, further avoiding his eyes. The tall one just kept staring at him. "Those are signs. We aim to aid in the symptoms."

"What *symptoms?*" Ian asked at the accusation.

Even Desire raised her eyebrows back at him in question. When he did not back down, she answered: "Lack of direction, hope, self-care, and the general self-loathing, for starters."

Her voice was familiar, but he couldn't place it in the moment. He also couldn't believe ignore the pull of their words. He did not believe them. He did not think he stood before a few of the seven deadly sins. That they would, and could, exist in front of him in this house. He also did not want to disbelieve it. Not believing meant returning to the emptiness. The hopelessness of a wandering path. Looking in her eyes he felt the connection of a distant life, of hope he couldn't let himself have.

"You mentioned there were others," Ian said, still holding firm to the obvious holes. "Where are they?"

"The others can be a bit...overbearing. In their own ways. And some you are too familiar with already." Dignity looked to the empty vodka bottle. "You will meet them in time."

"And which ones are you then?" Ian asked. He could list the seven deadly sins, names he had yet to hear from them. They had given him two different titles now— first under the umbrella of Spirits of the Cardinal Rapture, and then masquerading with individual names. All lies.

The one who called himself Passion opened his mouth, but Ian spoke first: "*a name I would actually know*," he seethed.

6

"Envy," said the woman.

"Lust," said the shorter man.

And then the last. "Pride."

Ian noticed his voice did have an air to it unlike the others. The man had carried himself with shoulders back and chin high since entering the house. There was a sense of confidence to him Ian had never quite possessed.

"And *why*, of all people, would I believe Spirits of the deadly sins are capable of helping me?" he asked.

"Who better to teach a poor man than a rich one? Who better to lead than those who can see the way? We are abundant in our knowledge. Some would say, to a fault," Pride finished.

He needed help, Ian knew that. The house was a start but he lacked so much he once had, and did not know how to get it back. He hated how his days went, and, even more so, who he had become. A man unable to get out of bed, no matter the desire held in his mind, who could never transfer it to his body. To create the energy needed to be who he once was. Where does one start when everything needs to be rebuilt? The same options were before him. He could call his parents, his brother, tell them the truth. He could try to do it on his own, little good that did the last time, or he could accept the help of these strangers.

Ian sighed, unable to voice his thoughts.

Pride took the resignation as acceptance. "Let us begin."

7

They let him sleep, eventually. Or tried to. Encumbered with his new information, sleep eluded him until the distant hours of the night.

Spirits. Demons. Angels. If one existed, so must the others. Ian still had difficulty believing, hoping he would wake to an empty house. One he could fill with vodka and microwave dinners. But he was forced to meet his new reality when he awoke to the sound of an Irish man singing. *Lust.*

He could hear them, before bed, as he lay there hoping it was all in his mind. Bickering on how they could fix him. He felt like he was back in Dr. Bardot's office, being examined except in the crudest of fashions. His lack of hygiene, his ill-fitting clothes, his thin and weightless hair. His gaunt frame and hollow, baggy eyes. How he looked years beyond his age and carried no weight in conversation. That he was a man who could be trodden over and to whom people were not keen to pay attention. They spoke of him like an object, like clay needing to be molded. His only solace was that they did not speak as if it were the clay's fault, but rather the task of the sculptor.

Morning now, their voices could still be heard echoing down the hall from where he left them, continuing to poke and prod his life like he was a lab rat in their experiment. The sound of a woman's voice carried to his room:

"…we have seen this before. What can we do that time will not fix on its own?"

"We have months, not years." The smooth voice of Pride. "And there is much we can do. Keep him alive, to begin with."

"How unfortunate it is, humans live only long enough to recognize their mistakes."

The lilt of an Irish accent cut through. "No human I've ever known was worse off after a round of fu—"

Ian couldn't listen any longer, the anxiety pressing on his bones. He rose and prepared himself to join the others, the shock of their candor sparking a realization. He threw on yesterday's clothes, making his way to the gallery of voices.

"How do you know what happened to me?" Ian asked without greeting.

"Good mornin' to you too, sunshine." Lust was wearing another signature tracksuit, this one a light blue with a crossed pattern, and a bucket hat pulled down just above his tinted glasses.

No one answered Ian and he wouldn't answer them, not until they told him what he was missing. They seemed to know everything about him before he even arrived.

"How do you know about me?" he repeated.

"The hospital," Pride said.

"They can't share my information. It's against HIPAA." Ian didn't know much about the medical industry but he knew that much.

Pride took a moment to think, the other two looking his way in deference.

"The entities that put us here are tied to the hospital," he said. "Our contracts belong to them, and in turn, the information on potential... *guests*, is awarded to us, to better complete our duties."

Ian thought about the file his appointed therapist had on him. "Dr. Bardot?"

"No. Now, if you're done with your questions, we have work to do."

47

"I'm not," Ian chided. "Do you three ever rest?"

He looked between them. They had all been up late into the night, the others later than him. If they slept, it was a handful of hours as most. Each looked not only to have been awake for hours, but fully dressed. Pride in another three-piece suit and Envy in something one might see on a fashion runway. None of it fit the aesthetic of the rundown home, sticking out like blood on snow.

"Yes. Although we can shift states, we are bound to human faculties," Pride answered, void of emotion. Ian asked it rhetorically, for the incessant bickering, but was happy with the earnest response before the fighting commenced.

"Why don't you just do what you did with the last person?" Ian asked, prodding for information. They had given no indication that there even was a previous tenant. They had given little indication of anything.

"That is not possible," Pride said. "You are not him."

"Thank you for another reminder that I'm lesser than," Ian said.

"That is not the point. You are dissimilar men, with disparate beliefs of your station, in a different place of life," Pride said, with mild agitation. "He was fifty-five years old and had been in prison since he was eighteen, with no knowledge or remembrance of how to live a life on the outside. Comprehension you possess."

"Was—was that a compliment?" Ian asked, and was answered with a glare.

"He needs to have a bit of the ol' in and out," said Lust.

"He needs time," said Envy.

"Minge 'ell do what time never could."

"Please. See reason," Envy said, casting her gaze to Pride.

"I'm still here," said Ian, annoyed they continued to speak as if he were not in the room.

"Let's be honest—that's only 'cause you failed to kill yourself."

7

They argued in the same way last night. Lust, disgustingly, argued the only way Ian would heal was through sex. Envy claimed a desire would eventually overcome Ian, getting him to act on his own behalf. Pride did not have an opinion at the time, managing the arguments of the other two.

"Quiet," said Pride. "I agree—with both of you."

Envy threw her hands up.

"Ian, you need your confidence restored. It will require assorted actions, and patience. We have but six months. Time will pass on its own," he said, eyeing the woman and leaving one option left.

"You want me to fuck my way out of depression?" asked Ian.

"It's always worked for—"

Lust was cut off by Pride. "*Quiet*," he repeated. "I want you to get comfortable with the idea of being with someone new."

"I don't want someone new," Ian said, and meant it. The past year, he could not stomach being with someone else. He did not want a spouse or a girlfriend or just someone to sleep with. He wanted what he had for the last year—to be left alone.

"That's why we're here," said Envy. "What clothes do you have to go out in?"

Ian looked down at himself. He was wearing his only pair of pants, and a plain T-shirt. A few spare shirts and the winter coat lay on the floor of his bedroom, but that was it. His other possessions and wardrobe had been taken with the repossessed house.

When Ian looked back up, Envy was mortified but tried to fix it with a smile. "We have quite the to-do list then."

Ian looked to the stack of bills someone had gathered on the kitchen counter, after he dropped them last night. "I don't have the money for that."

The ambulance, stitches, and overnight stay in the hospital already a burden to him, clothes were the least of his worries. Dr. Bardot's continued work might be free, but that did not fix the empty bank account—a negative balance last he checked—and lack of income.

"That can be fixed," she said. "You will meet with Gio in the morning. In the meantime, I will cover the expense."

Gio. That was the second time he had heard that name, its mention bringing about a shift in Pride's demeanor. If Ian wasn't mistaken, he could have sworn it was a flash of guilt.

"Who is that?" he asked.

"Greed," said Pride. "He goes by his human name exclusively, as he is mostly in their presence. Do not call him anything but."

"How will he help?"

"Are you hard of hearin'? He's the embodiment of *Greed*," said Lust, drawing out the last word.

Ian ignored him, looking back to Pride and wondering if the meeting would happen at that very table. "Does he live here?" he asked.

"He used to. He has since moved downtown."

Ian felt uneasy at this. *He had to seek out a demon?* Living here was one thing, with those actively trying to help. Why would Greed—Gio—move out if he wanted the same thing they did? Ian had not asked for help from any of them. They had volunteered, and he found himself still hesitant at accepting. Seeking them out was not what he would choose.

Pride picked up on his unease. "He is bound here like the rest of us. He will fulfill his duties. And," Pride pushed the stack of mounting bills toward Ian, "he can help with these."

Ian stared at them in contempt. "They're not his problem."

"Try not to take this the way you are going to—but *everything* about you is our problem."

Pride did not say it with hatred or pity. He said it as a statement of fact. Ian was their *directive*, as they had said. Either his life got better, or they stayed here. The Spirits might not look at him as a burden, and yet, Ian could not help but feel one.

"He's just going to pay this?" Ian asked, and was met with a laugh.

"Doubtful, but he has much knowledge. You can ask him about how to handle the bills while inquiring about employment," said Envy.

"And after that?" Ian asked.

"The fun begins."

8

Ian peered from the corner window, looking over the dull gridline of lanes below. It had to be one of the highest offices in one of the tallest buildings in the city, and yet stood no more than twenty stories tall. Staring at the street far below, he raised his eyes little by little, passing downtown, the suburbs, the tram and track lines, out to the boroughs where he now resided. Wealth and poverty, so easy to spot, street after street in the decidedly segregated lines—more houses than not with chain-link fences and parking pads over driveways. The homeless he passed on the way and the few city parks; little more than underdeveloped squares of grass.

Ian was waiting for Greed—Gio—in the lobby of the Spirit's office, accompanied by the secretary keenly ignoring him behind her desk. He assumed his clothing and demeanor gave away that he was not a normal client. If the office were seen from above like Ian saw the city now, it would be one island of noticeable wealth in a sea of poverty. Perhaps the most lavish office within 100 miles. Wood lined the walls in fine, bold lines like that of mansions from the Gilded Age. Marble floors and iron railings made their way throughout the floor occupied by Mammon Group, the private equity fund founded by Gio, according to the plaque on the wall. It hung next to a framed article with a centerpiece image of a man he could only assume was Greed.

BUSINESS WEEKLY
Out of the basement and into the penthouse. *Giovanni Costa, a first-generation immigrant from the shores of Calabria, had humble beginnings as a cold caller in a boiler room operation seventeen years ago this June. He now owns Mammon Group, a private equity fund focused on the "health and sustainability" of mid-level corporations, though many speculate on the ethics of the operation. The resident tycoon has garnered a reputation as a brutal job slasher but effective businessman, purchasing companies in private acquisition, selling off profitable divisions, and closing the less economically suitable. Though morally divisive, the tactic has also proven viable in turning around corporations that would otherwise become defunct, something the owner himself preaches as gospel.*

"Look at Fisker Lumber," Gio said in our interview in November, "a Mammon group acquisition made last year. At the time, a company on the brink of financial collapse. Less than twelve months later, we're happy to report the highest earnings in two decades. Critics can focus on the necessary cutbacks made to achieve that, or they can focus on the livelihoods we preserved."

Gio goes on to tell us that Mammon Group's focus in the coming years will be on local economies, in an attempt to impact the wellbeing of those closer to home. Time will tell if this proves fortunate.

(Pictured: Giovanni Costa for the cover of Business Weekly)

Seventeen years. Ian was wondering to himself if that was how long they had all been there, or just Greed, when Gio came walking out to meet him, identical to the photo on the wall. The man was much like the others; his look and demeanor suited the Spirit he embodied, matched even more so by the occupation he chose. Thick slicked-back hair mounted on a middle-aged face with sharp beady eyes. Taller than Lust, but not near the height of Pride, he looked...dependable, Ian thought. Handsome but not showing off, though his face was blank as he stopped short of Ian.

"Not exactly New York," Ian said, by way of a question.

Greed looked out his direction, noticing the same city view. "There's money to be made anywhere," he said. "Follow me."

"So you know why I'm here," Ian replied, walking past the aloof secretary and into the office. Gio didn't pay mind to him again until the doors were firmly shut. The office was as opulent as the waiting area, only more personal. Local accolades, newspaper articles, and Forbes clippings sat on the floor-to-ceiling inlays behind the grand desk, telling the story of Greed's last seventeen years. On the opposite wall sat bookshelves filled to the brim, and a mounted rolling ladder. It was pristine, the opposite of how his counterparts lived in every way.

The finely tuned businessman went to his desk and stood before it like an altar. Greed. Ian was meeting the Spirit of Greed in one of the most lavish rooms he had ever stepped foot in, and he felt the pull. The desire to live like this, to have more than he could spend. He had lived well, once, but nothing like this.

"And what do you expect me to do for you?" Gio asked, pulling him back down to earth.

"Good to meet you, too," Ian said.

"I have another client meeting in fifteen."

"I'm a client?"

"The person before you was a client. The person after you is a client. You are—here," Greed said. "Make the most of it."

"Are you aware of who I am?"

"Yes."

"Are you aware of my—situation?"

"I can assume," Gio said, unfurling his arms and apparently gesturing to the appearance of Ian that did not meet his standard.

"You really are all related," Ian said, dully.

"We are no more kin than you are to Marcy," he gestured again, this time to the closed doors between them and the aloof secretary. "Ask your questions and leave."

This is what Ian did not want. To beg for the help of one of these demons, let alone one who could fix so many of his problems. All of his problems. The others could not fix what Ian had broken, but Greed—Greed could solve his financial issue and return him to the unabated peace of solitude.

"I—I don't have any questions," Ian said. "They just told me to come see you."

Gio took a sharp breath in, his face pulling tight. "I suggest you create some. The quality of your life and output is determined by the quality of the questions you ask."

Ian's hands slumped down to his sides. The others, for all their faults, had a plan in place for him. A guide, it seemed, to assist. He had assumed Greed would as well. Heat was rising to his face, of shame, of frustration, when he felt the crinkle of papers in pocket, remembering what they were.

"What's the first thing you'd do if you were broke and had to pay these?" He pulled the bills out from his pocket and waved them.

"I wouldn't be broke," Greed said, taking a seat.

Ian breathed in, closing his eyes and trying to keep his composure. He hated these people. These demons. "That's not an answer."

"I wouldn't pay it, either," Greed said.

"You don't even know what it is," Ian said.

"Unless it's a student loan payment, it doesn't matter what it is. I'd wait about three, three and a half years. Your credit's already tanked, I presume?" Gio asked and didn't give him time to answer. "Let it go to collections. Let that collections company sell it to another, who sells it to another, and settle on the debt in three and a half years for pennies on the dollar." Greed wasn't looking at him, as if Ian was on the other end of a phone call waiting to be hung up on.

"That seems like a very specific amount of time," Ian clipped, fishing for more information.

"It is. Collectors can only come after you for four."

"Then why pay at all?"

"Didn't you use to work in finance? Greed asked. "No wonder they fired you." So he too knew about the past.

"I managed brokerage accounts for old people. WHY would I pay it at that specific time?" Ian asked, frustration mounting.

"Because you eventually want it off your credit," Greed said, sorting through paperwork as if the meeting was over.

This made sense, if it was true. With the foreclosure of his last house, his credit was far from good standing. His bank accounts had also been forcibly shut down given his negative balances over the past year. Ian knew he wouldn't be in a place to buy another home anytime soon, and a loan for a car was the least of his worries. Medical debt could go on the back burner for years if poor credit was all that was at stake.

"Is that all?" Greed asked.

"What? No. I—I need a job." The real reason he was here. Money.

"We're not hiring," said Greed.

"Pride said you..." Ian began, but Gio's face tightened and cut him off.

"As usual, Pride promised something he can't deliver."

"Isn't it your job to help?" Ian asked cautiously. If a word of what the other had said were true, Greed was as far up a creek as them all. Either he helped, or he was stuck here.

Cold beady eyes peered up, black irises meeting Ian's own. "You are not my job, and your time is up."

As if she had heard every word, the secretary was in the room before Gio was done speaking. With a closed door in his face, the meeting was over.

8

Envy beat him to where they had agreed to meet, at the corner outside a place called Lou's Tavern. It occupied the southwest corner of the open town square. Businesses lined the area and, regardless of the poor winter weather, people walked about. With each other, with their dogs, by themselves.

When Ian arrived, he found her alone on a park bench.

She was breathtaking. He still wasn't used to seeing her, and the oddity of her beauty was confirmed as he noticed the passersby looking as well. Man or woman, old or young, they all stole their glances at her. Whether they walked away or toward her, they looked. Whether she noticed or not, he could not tell.

Walking up, Ian took the seat next to Envy. "May I ask you a question?" he said and she chuckled, juxtaposed to his meeting with Gio an hour before.

"Humans are funny. Was that not one already?" she asked.

"It means—"

"I know. It still perplexes me though."

It was difficult, Ian found, to remember who they were. *What* they were. They talked like humans and looked like humans, even if the most attractive among them. They acted like humans, mostly. But they were Spirits. Not of this world and here for reasons Ian still didn't fully understand.

"Did you choose this form? Did you all choose the bodies you are in?" Ian asked, and she smiled again.

"You all ask the same questions each time. This is why it perplexes me. You are each so different, and yet so alike," she said. "Yes, we were granted the ability to choose our forms, and the ability to change them as well."

So many questions he could ask from such routine statements, and yet Ian asked, "Why?"

Envy tilted her head. "That one is new, actually," she said at this simple question, and seemed to be mulling it over. "Our recompense can only be carried out if we are successful. We were given the ability to choose our features so that we could pick forms that best deliver the desired outcome."

"That explains why you can pick the body, but why the ability to change them?"

"Our sentences on Earth are…long. Some longer than others. We needed the ability to blend in over time."

This shocked him. He knew, instinctively, she was not human, and therefore would not be the youthful age she emitted. He hadn't considered exactly how far off he could be.

"How—how old are you?" he asked, this question drawing the loudest and most genuine laugh from her yet. When she was able to answer, she said, "We do not measure our existence in time that you would understand. However, I have been on Earth for two hundred and thirty-seven years."

Two hundred and thirty-seven years. He didn't know what he expected when he asked, but hearing it made it all too real, the new questions starting to form in his mind and him asking them as fast as they did. *What did you do? What about the others? Have you always been in that house? How long will you be here?* To his dismay, she did not answer.

"Questions for another time. We are here to talk about you," she said, ending the line of questions and her demeanor shifting just as fast.

Envy turned back to the town square and the people walking about. "I come here sometimes, just to watch," she said, pointing across the grounds in the direction most traffic flowed. "There's a business park on the other side, there. You get all kinds walking through here. Have you ever been?"

"No. I don't think so," Ian said.

"Does it not look familiar?"

"Should it?" he asked, and glanced around at the town center once again. It looked like—a park. There was a large field, walkways cut through to leave separated swaths of grass. Areas for children to play, and a fountain at the center. A large oak tree occupied the leftmost corner, its barren branches waiting for the leaves to return and shower the field with shade.

He did not notice it at first. The day was gloomy where the vision was previously bright. The grass covered in leaves and residue snow where it was previously lush with green. It was the park Envy used in the visions she showed him, except there were no children this time, no woman in white. The woman from the vision.

Difficult to discern on a winter day, Ian was used to seeing the setting with fogged edges in the brightness of summer. Now, it looked so— barren, in comparison. Ian felt the dread and the pain rise up, more so than the lingering hollow that usually accompanied him. For a moment, he had felt happy, excited, discovering the world that these Spirits possessed. In a moment, it drained from him.

"Why are we here?" Ian asked.

"I told you—to watch," she said. "What do you see?"

Ian looked around, encumbered by flashes of the vision, glimmering in and out of the bright disposition of desired hope and happiness, to the dark presence of now. A man in a suit, his tie tucked between the buttons of his white oxford as he ate his lunch. A woman, hat on and headphones in as she ran with her German Shepherd. He saw people with purpose, who had things to do and who enjoyed doing them. He saw people he used to be, and did not answer her.

"You want, Ian. No matter how much you shove it down, you want for things. You can hide it from most people. But you cannot hide it from me," she said, gently placing a hand on his cheek to turn his face.

If it were anyone else, any other Spirit, it would have been too much. He could not pull away from her and her silver stare full of knowing.

"I see it in your eyes. To others, the eyes carry the sorrow of your heart. But sorrow is nothing more than desire unfulfilled."

"How am I supposed to want, when all I have ever done is lost?" Ian asked, pain rising at a rate he could not quell.

"You will allow yourself to dream again, after you mourn what you have lost." She removed her hand, turning back to the park, leaving Ian to sort himself; he had more questions than answers.

"How did it go with Gio?" she asked after one moment of silence turned into many. It took an additional moment for Ian to recognize the name. *Greed.*

"I can see why Pride kicked him out," Ian said, assuming as much. Pride had bristled at the mere mention of the man. Gio, in turn, had kicked Ian out just after Pride was brought up.

Envy hesitated. "He didn't. Gio left on his own."

Ian looked at her, another question on his face that she recognized without him asking.

"He and Pride had a disagreement, after the last subject we assisted."

"What happened?" he asked.

"I don't think that's for me to say," she said and changed the subject. "Regardless, Gio should have helped."

"If he is your idea of 'help', I might as well learn to tie a noose."

"You shouldn't joke about that," she said, eyes darting to him.

They contained a suspicion and an accusation. A look he was familiar with. *Fear.* If he killed himself, they would not get credit. They would still be here on Earth serving their sentence, forced to help the next person, having wasted however long on him. A pang of bitterness rose hot on his tongue. They might be helping him, but it was not charity if it was forced.

8

"We will handle Gio," she continued. "For now, I will cover the expenses. Let's go."

⸶

Malls always had a unique sound, as if they emitted their own atmosphere. They were noisy—echoey, but equally tranquil and subdued. A mixture of foot traffic, water fountains, and a flurry of conversation.

"I hate malls," Ian said.

"Everyone hates malls."

"Then why are we here?"

"Convenience," she said. "It wouldn't be my first choice, but we don't have time to fly you to Paris."

"Or the money," Ian said, lamenting the conversation. He intended to turn down Envy's offer to front the money, not wanting to get further in debt, and he suspected she knew that. It was one thing to owe a hospital or a credit card company, but he did not want to owe a demon. He also didn't know what choice he had.

"You were successful in your old life, were you not?"

"Modestly. I was never a millionaire, if that's your question."

As they rode the escalators to the main floor, he thought to the home he once owned and the furniture they filled it with. The two vehicles in the garage not six months old. The suits and watches—and the debt. He made good money, but he also leveraged debt. They chose to enjoy the money, he and his wife, spending instead of saving. Having been so young he always assumed he would make more. Now, having lost his licenses, he didn't know how that would be possible.

"I have faith you are good for it," she said.

Faith. An interesting word for a demon.

"How do you make money, anyway? Do any of you even have jobs?" Ian asked, changing the subject. Her clothes alone had to cost a fortune and he was yet to see her repeat wearing so much as a bracelet.

Envy stopped and turned. "You'd be surprised what can be acquired when you live to two hundred."

He waited for her to continue, but they had arrived. The shop they stood in front of had floor-to-ceiling transparent glass panels, showing rows of black chairs and blacker sinks. It was not full, but what people did occupy the store were entirely women.

"A salon?" he asked in disbelief.

"They'll treat you better than a barber," she said, opening the door. The room turned to look at who had entered and they were greeted by a tall blonde with pointed features and sculpted eyebrows, her outfit second only to Envy's.

"Evelyn, love! How I've missed you," she said, a hairbrush waving in her hand as she crossed the room straight toward them.

"*Evelyn?*" Ian asked in a hushed tone.

"Gio's the only one who gets a name?" she whispered before turning back to embrace the woman striding up.

"Savannah, so good to see you," Envy said, hugging her and stopping with a gasp, "Where did you get those earrings? I must have them."

"If *you* want them, I must be doing something right," she winked and caught sight of Ian. "Another client?"

A client. Of course, this was where she'd have brought the others they had assisted as well. How many of them had there been?

"Ian," Envy said as way of introduction, and he shook the woman's hand. "We're looking for a full makeover. Can you help?"

Savannah didn't hesitate and didn't ask permission. Ian's shoulders shot back in defense as she reached up to run her fingers through his long greasy hair, his scruff, his eyebrows, moving it every which way and walking around the back of him, occasionally standing on her toes to get a better angle. Ian tried turning with her, self-conscious of the state he knew he was in, but she maneuvered him as she wished and wasn't shy about it. When Savannah was done, she held her hands out

62

8

in front of her as if covered in grime.

"Workable. Are we a fan of the neckbeard?" she asked Envy, both women turning to look at him fully.

"Wouldn't know. I've never seen him without it," Envy said.

"I see. Well, carte blanche?"

Ian felt like a cow at an auction, fully feeling the lack of autonomy in his immediate future but not sure he could or even should speak up. The judgment and potential unknowns of what was to come made him nervous.

"I wouldn't come here if I didn't trust you," Envy said, waving a hand to continue.

"Well then, we'll start with a wash."

Over the next two hours, Savannah and her assistants washed, dried, washed again, cut, trimmed, shaved, and even waxed parts of him. Envy excused herself, stating she would use the time for his new wardrobe, which further baffled Ian as he wasn't sure how she could pick out clothes for him without him trying them on.

Though the appointment was long, he had little time to adjust to what was happening to him as he looked down and saw nearly foot-long strands of hair fall to the tarp that covered his frame. He was only taken out of the daze by the wax-covered popsicle sticks stuck up his nose and yanked out in a way that brought tears to his eyes. Even at the height of his wealth, he had never sought this level of grooming and never wanted to again.

When it was done, Savannah whirled the chair around toward a mirror. "Voilà!" she said, enthused at her work.

What Ian saw looking back at him was a face he did not recognize, but eyes that had not changed.

9

"Beards grow back, don't they?" Envy asked.

They were headed back to the house, car full of black bags hanging from the headrests. His new wardrobe, he assumed. Ian looked quite different, if Envy's mostly positive reaction was any indication. She seemed to be excited about him no longer looking homeless, but regretted the lack of facial hair. The small pang in his chest reminded him of the adjustments he'd tried to make in his marriage that went unappreciated.

"They do."

"And roughly how long does that take?" she asked, eyes dancing between his clean face and slicked-back side part. She smiled but the rest of her features did not. He'd never worn his hair this way, mostly letting short bangs hang on his forehead in his younger years, and thought it suited him, but he too missed the sheltering bristle of his beard, he thought, his fingers rising to the foreign feeling of bare skin. Though that was not where his mind lay.

"Back at the mall, you said Spirits of your kind have faith," Ian said, ignoring her question. "What is it you believe in?"

Envy, not surprised by the question, only at the abrupt shift in his demeanor, replied evenly: "We believe the unabashed engrossment of all that free will entails is not a damnable offense."

Ian considered this, and what it implied.

9

"You think there shouldn't be sins?"

She took a moment to ponder the question. "There are limits to indulgence, and those far bounds are sins. They are not, however, the end of forgiveness, but rather the beginning."

"That's a convenient belief system for someone like you," Ian observed as they rounded the corner to Naferty Lane, the house coming into view. He didn't intend to insult the one person who he felt at ease with, but couldn't overlook it either. Evelyn didn't have time to answer him before they were met with an unrecognized car, far too nice for their neighborhood, parked at their curb.

Pride and Greed stood on the front porch, awkward distance between the two and having a heated discussion.

Envy got out first, in front of him on the path to the house, and Ian overheard Gio as he passed.

"Mind your fucking business," he told her before adding to Ian, not bothering to look at him, "See you on Monday. Wear a suit."

Pride turned to enter the house.

"What the hell was that?" Ian asked.

Envy looked at him with sympathy in her eyes. "Our own problems," she replied.

"That's not good enough," Ian said, tired of their insufficient answers.

"I told you we'd handle Gio," she said, "and we did. Leave it at that."

They unpacked the car in silence, taking the black clothing bags to his room and laying them on the floor. There were dozens of them, some bags light and airy, others requiring both hands to carry, stuffed with God knows what Envy had purchased. Ian hadn't noticed the long boxes in the rear of the car—clothing racks for his new wardrobe, she told him.

"How much was all of this?" Ian asked, anxious to hear the amount he now owed to yet another party.

She patted her dress, feigning a search. "Hmm—I seem to have misplaced the receipt."

"Evelyn..." Ian said, deliberately using her human moniker. He didn't want to pay the bill, but he also didn't want to be in a different kind of debt.

She whirled. *"Do not* use my name like that."

"Don't lie to me; this is worth thousands."

"We're not allowed to lie, remember?" She spun, showing off her pocketless blouse and a sardonic smile. "Do you see a receipt?"

Ian wasn't satisfied, wondering what exactly he would owe in the future if it wasn't to be money. They were interrupted by Lust bounding down the stairs and taking in Ian's new look.

"Who's this moderately handsome stranger?" Lust cheered and was met with silence. "Kiddin'. At least now it's a face I can work with. Should've kept the beard, though."

"How kind of you."

"My pleasure, boyo. So, when are we celebratin'?"

Ian eyed him suspiciously. *"What* are we celebrating?" he asked, setting down the final box on the kitchen counter.

"Haven't you heard? You've got a new job," Lust smiled.

So that was why Greed was there. Whatever happened between them, this was the outcome.

"Doing what?" Ian asked, weariness in his voice. Employment was a stipulation of remaining here, though he had assumed he'd have some say in what it would be.

"That is up to Gio, unfortunately, and it is not a celebration," Pride said, dimming the smile on Lust's face. "With our limited time, we think it best to take advantage of the upcoming weekend."

"With what?" Ian asked again, frustration mounting. They were not his personal keepers, nor was he a pet for them to decide where he went and when he went there.

"The other day we discussed the idea of you becoming comfortable with the prospect of another human companion. We will be going out," Pride said.

"*Human companions* are not pets you buy at a store. And I told you I didn't want that," Ian shot.

"Evelyn seems to disagree," said Pride, and Ian turned to her. Apology was written on her face. "She says it is what you dream of."

The vision. It was not his dream, though. He had never had that dream before moving into this house. For some reason, that was not what struck him the most.

"You call each other your human names?" Ian asked.

"We do, and so will you—in public, at least."

"And what am I to call you two?" he looked at Lust and back to Pride.

"He is Louie. You are to call me Pearce. We will be accompanying you tomorrow night," Pride said, moving on.

Ian felt a tinge of worry at the prospect of being alone with the two he liked the least. "I want her there," Ian gestured to Envy.

"It is better that she stays," said Pride, setting his jaw and offering nothing further.

Ian hated how Pride said things so matter of factly. As if his word were law simply because he said it was so.

"Why?" Ian pushed back.

Lust—Louie—cut in. "Take a look at her."

Ian didn't, turning to Lust instead.

"You think anyone wants to compete with that? She's beautiful, which is the exact reason why you don't want her around."

Although he did not want to, Ian relented. Envy was possibly the most beautiful woman he had ever seen, in person or otherwise. He doubted it could be mistaken that they were together, but regardless, it wouldn't help. However, Ian still found himself wanting her there. She was a calming presence, whereas the other two set him on edge. Pride was a wall waiting to be crashed into, and Lust was simply unnerving.

Envy gave him a reassuring smile. "I may not be invited, but perhaps there is a more desirable combination," she said, a hint of mystery and desire to be trusted in her words.

Before Ian could inquire further, his phone rang. He fumbled for his pockets, pulled out the phone and looked down to see the caller ID: *Mom—Home*

Ian's heart raced and his mind blanked, still not ready to have this conversation. He sent it to voicemail, as he had every day since. He looked up to a quiet and still room, all eyes on the device in his hand.

"You can't ignore them forever," Evelyn said quietly.

"I won't have to," replied Ian, grabbing what he could of the bags and heading to his room.

10

Ian woke to the sound of bass drums. It was quiet at first. A steady, moving beat of a passing car that grew progressively louder through the walls. It was dark out, and a peek at his phone showed 3 in the morning. His eyes burned deeply on the two hours of sleep he'd managed, having been kept up by the noises coming from Lust's room. He'd brought a woman, Michelle, back from somewhere. Ian only knew the name due to Lust's unfortunate cries of pleasure, hers following shortly after. He thankfully couldn't hear them now.

As he lay his head back down, Ian noticed the rhythmic thump had stopped traveling at a halt outside the house. It played at an even volume before cutting out, and he was once again met with the silence of the night.

Then came the creak of the front door.

He shouldn't get up, he told himself. Since Ian's learning of the Spirits, they had been less shy of their whereabouts. One could be heard doing something or other almost constantly, though it was usually Envy bringing in a new piece of furniture to try out for the day or Lust indulging in his new flavor of the evening. At this hour, they'd all be asleep. He wasn't exactly sure how they got to and from the house, with only Pride's SUV between them but he knew one thing.

Lust was in his room.

Ian crawled out of bed, grabbing the fire poker he'd kept at his bedside since the frightful night with Pride. He moved barefoot down the hall, headed toward the noise and shallow light of the kitchen. The bass of the car was now replaced by the off-tune beatboxing of a voice he didn't recognize.

"Ba-da-dadada-da-ta- dadada-da ta..."

It grew louder as Ian rounded the corner and stared at the most muscular back he had ever seen. Blond hair collided with dark skin on a man wearing a bright gym stringer—an inch-thick piece of cloth keeping it together in the back, his protruding lat muscles not letting his arms lay flat at his sides. The man wore high-top shoes, and his shorts were busting at the seams as he was dancing his way across the kitchen, kicking his feet to the made-up sounds. Ian finally noticed the headphones emitting the same beat in a high-pitched frequency.

As the man kicked low one more time and spun, he caught sight of Ian and knocked the headphones off his head in one fluid motion, hanging them around his neck and bringing his hands up to fight.

"Who are you?" Ian practically yelled, iron poker raised to his shoulder like a bat.

"I live here, who the fuck are *you*?" the man shot back, bouncing on his heels.

They stared at each other. If this man claimed to live here, Ian only had a few options for who he could be. Wrath, maybe. The man certainly had a temper. Definitely not Sloth. A human?

"Which one are you?" Ian asked.

The man squinted at him, not giving in. "What do you know?"

"I know plenty."

"Define plenty." The man's eyes got wide, fists still raised.

Ian thought for a second. If he was one of them, this would be completely fine. Normal, almost. If he was wrong, and this was the lover of one of the Spirits, he might sound borderline insane. He risked it.

10

"I know Envy lives in the attic, and Lust is a short Irishman," Ian said, squinting his own eyes.

The muscular man visibly relaxed, his fighting hands opening in greeting, before lowering them and turning to look in the fridge. "Oh, you must be Ian. I thought you'd be older." He turned around, tearing off the top of a yogurt container and tasting it with his finger. "Name's Gavin."

"The Spirit of..." Ian trailed off in question, met with a cocky know-it-all grin from the stranger.

"I believe the old magistrates and white-wearing kiddy touchers call me Gluttony."

Ian's jaw fell open. *No. It couldn't be.* Ian knew little of the seven deadly sins, though he supposed he knew as much as anyone. Gluttony was a Spirit of indulgence. A Spirit that lacked self-control. But this man was lean, toned, and chiseled. His arms were the size of Ian's thighs, and his thighs were as round as Ian's torso.

While Ian stared, Gavin finished off the yogurt, opening more cabinets, apparently not satisfied with his findings. Met with silence, he turned to find Ian still slack-jawed. "What?"

"I thought you'd be fat," Ian replied after a moment, finally lowering the poker.

Gluttony choked out a laugh. "What're you here for?" he asked, resuming his search.

"Didn't have anywhere else to go," said Ian. It wasn't entirely true but it was unfortunately his best option.

"That's the case for everyone who comes here. What did you *do*?"

"Shouldn't you know? Everyone else already does."

"I don't read all that nonsense," Gluttony said. "Evelyn called last night and said I was needed. Didn't think you'd already be here."

"This how you greet all the guests?"

"Just the ones who ambush me half naked with a weapon," Gluttony said, and Ian looked down at himself. He was more than half naked, sporting only his underwear and the iron poker, one covering significantly more skin than the other.

"Tried to kill myself," Ian answered and, to his surprise, received another laugh.

"Awfully funny for someone on the brink of death."

"Awfully toned for someone with an insatiable appetite," Ian said with thin eyes.

The comment was not only about his appearance, but what the man was currently doing. All the food Ian had purchased was being laid out on the counter. Microwave mac and cheese, TV dinners, and ramen noodles.

"Who bought this shit?" Gluttony said, ignoring his statement and throwing another pack of convenience store food on the countertop.

"I did," Ian said defensively.

Gluttony turned around to eye him again, Ian feeling the gaze on the duality of his too small frame and protruding gut. "You eat like shit," he said, turning back to finish whatever he had started.

"If you're going to eat all that, I expect you to replace it."

Gluttony frowned, looking at the pile of food and pointing, "I'm not eating this and neither should you. It's useless."

"And what use are you, exactly?" It sounded more accusatory than Ian intended but he wasn't sure how else to word it at this hour. As best Ian could tell, each Spirit had their own agenda for him. If Gluttony was here, a self-improvement task was right around the corner. It was in every word they said, every task and alteration to his life.

The man grinned. He was always grinning. It looked natural but it unnerved Ian—no one was that happy naturally. The ones who looked it had faked it or bought it and he wasn't sure which was worse.

"Fancy a run in the morning?"

Ian audibly groaned and began heading back to his room, entirely too tired for this. "Oh, get fucked. If that's why Envy called you, she's going to be disappointed."

"That's not why she called," Gluttony said to his back.

Ian turned around, more curious than annoyed.

"You will work out with me, one way or another. But that's not why I'm here."

"Then why are you here?" Ian asked, ignoring the command he had no intention of following.

"We're going out tomorrow. You, me, and the Irishman," Gluttony replied, that smile still pulling at his lips.

⸸

The night was already off to a terrible start.

Before leaving, Lust and Gluttony had insisted on a "fashion show" for Ian's new clothes. No one could agree on what was conventionally attractive, or appropriate, as Gluttony wanted him to dress in a full three-piece suit, though he himself was wearing a simple black T-shirt, and Lust kept asking "Do you have anythin' else?" after each outfit Ian tried.

Had Envy been in the house, Ian would've just worn what she liked, but she was off to a trade show for the weekend looking at new furniture. Eventually Ian told them both to wait in the car and settled on a dark button-up and jeans.

Now they were pulling into a nightclub parking lot, Gluttony driving and Lust bouncing in his seat while poorly singing along at the top of his lungs to a catchy song on the radio.

Gluttony was singing along too, though much closer to the true pitch, when Ian was scolded by Lust, "You gotta get your energy up. You're killin' me here," he said, turning down the music.

"Your voice has been killing deaf animals for the past 15 miles. My empathy lies with them."

"Oh, like you'da rather sat in silence?"

"I think he'd rather be at home," Gluttony said after Ian didn't respond.

"Well, he's not at home and he's not givin' us much to work with," Lust said, hands rising in frustration, "So I need a little energy from the lad."

Lust turned to Ian then. "I don't think I've seen you smile yet. You have all your teeth?" he asked, baring all of his as if at the dentist.

Ian just opened the car door to head inside.

⸸

He had avoided places like this throughout his twenties. It was one of the many reasons he loved being married—not having to be in a club. Some people went to clubs to party, some to not feel alone, and some went to meet people. He didn't understand why clubs were dating arenas then, and now in his thirties and never having been clubbing before, he understood it even less.

The only solace was that Lust knew the arenas in this city well, and chose one more suited to his age. Men and women from their late twenties up until their fifties, from what he could see in the poor lighting conditions, roamed the bar, side lounges, and dance floor, prompting a question for Lust.

"Why'd you pick that body?" Ian asked. Lust was a handsome man by any conventional standards, but not near the attractiveness of Pride, Envy, or even Greed or Gluttony for that matter. Having learned they could choose their own bodies, and even alter them over time, it didn't make sense for a Spirit of Lust to choose this one, let alone one under six feet tall.

"Whatcha mean, boyo?" asked Lust, apparently unaware of his poor decision, but as Ian raised his eyebrows in disbelief, Lust cracked and flashed a smile. "Game's only fun if it's competitive," he practically yelled, though he was less than a foot away. "First body I was in, that thing was chiseled by Michelangelo himself. A face from the gods with two full hams on the rear and an aubergine up front," Lust said, making the other two both happy for the blaring music, by the look on Gluttony's face. "But, I think I spread more syphilis that year than the King. Quite frankly, it was too easy."

Ian didn't know where to start, at the hatred for Lust's further lack of tact or at the self-pitying life of a man too handsome.

"That must have been tough," he said, to which Lust laughed.

"I've been in every make and model you can imagine—and done much more with far less." He eyed Ian up and down accusingly. "This one's a good middle ground, I figure," Lust said, wiping his hands down his legs and chest when he spoke, as if double checking and agreeing with the hardware he had chosen. "Gotta earn it—keeps me sharp."

Now looking back at the prowling grounds called a dance floor from the second-story balcony, Ian wished they *had* stayed home. The room was filled with some men better-looking than himself and some not. Lust could claim his body gave him a disadvantage all he wanted, but with the square jawline, patchless 5 o'clock shadow and the accent to boot, he was shooting fish in a barrel as far as Ian was concerned. And witnessed it as well. Without noticing, Lust had left his side and was spotted moving through the crowd on his own as Ian and Gluttony watched from above.

"You don't want to join him?" Ian asked Gluttony, who was also no longer there. Gluttony had found a server a few yards from their section, and appeared to be buying shots. This was confirmed when he returned, offering one to Ian. "It'll loosen you up."

"I don't want it," Ian said.

"That's not what I hear," Gluttony replied, pulling the offered glass back and drinking both in quick succession. His large frame could probably handle the alcohol well, though Ian wondered how this fit with his diet. "I hear you drink it by the bottle."

75

"I drink it when I want it, and didn't you accuse me of poor eating habits?"

"Cheat day," Gluttony said, buying two more from a passing waitress carrying Jello shots.

Ian shook his head in disbelief at the bounce in logic from last night to now, turning back to find Lust.

His small frame was surprisingly easy to find in the plaid tracksuit, and he had moved from one side of the room to the other, a faint smile on his face. As he walked he made remarks to women of all ages and every look. Some would outright ignore him, pretending they didn't hear. Some would smile back, place a hand on his arm, his chest, move in to whisper back in his ear before Lust—Louie—moved on to the next. He never stopped for more than ten seconds and even occasionally would point up at Ian when talking to some of the noticeably less attractive ones. Now having surveyed the room, Lust made his way back to the second-story balcony where Ian and Gluttony awaited.

Ian felt he knew his looks well, and felt even more confident he was in the bottom half of the options presented throughout the room. The men years beyond his age were in better shape, and by the look of how they were spending money, significantly better off. His new clothes weighed heavy on his back and he was suddenly very aware that his nose itched.

"*Stop that,*" a deep, knowing voice said. Ian didn't hear it, he thought it, reverberating through his mind the same way it did that day in Dr. Bardot's office. The day Pride entered his mind. Ian turned to his right, to Gluttony, who was staring at him with a blank expression.

"How are you doing that?" Ian asked in shock.

Gluttony shrugged. "It's easy to get into human minds, especially when you're acting like that. You're practically inviting us in."

"What?"

"You're being self-conscious; self-pitying. It's all over your face," said

Gluttony. "It's an indulgence that radiates off you like the fear of a child. You need to stop."

Ian looked at him incredulously. "How am I supposed to just stop being self-conscious?"

"By definition. You stop thinking about it."

"*Great fucking advice.* How many centuries did you work on that line?" he said, feeling heat in his face and turning back to the crowd. They were practically yelling at each other but no one seemed to notice. The music rattled the floor, the railing. How anyone enjoyed being in such a place was beyond him.

Lust had arrived, approaching from his left, putting an arm around Ian's shoulders and sending a shiver down his spine. "Plenty of options tonight, gentlemen. Pick one."

Ian shrugged the arm off. "Christ. *Pick one?* It's not a farmer's market."

"Don't use that name," Lust said, "and yeah, it is."

Ian regarded him with the same look he had given Gluttony moments before. "They're people, Lust."

"*Louie,*" he corrected, "and yeah, they are. People who are here to feel wanted. Some come just to dance, some might be here because their lonely friend dragged them along. But the majority are here because some dope like you is here. And they're waitin' to be wooed."

Ian stared out into the crowd, saying nothing but holding defeat on his face. He knew he had to. Knew the only way to meet someone was to talk to them. But what would he—

"You just go right up and tell her she has nice tits."

"*I will not!*" shot Ian. "Are you insane? You don't just say that to a stranger."

"I just did, about a baker's dozen times. It's not about what you say, it's about how you say—" Lust started before Gluttony cut him off.

"What are you comfortable saying?" he asked. "What would you say

77

if we weren't here?"

Ian thought he wouldn't say anything if they weren't here. He wouldn't be here. He'd be at home, doing whatever mindless activity he could find to pass the time, knowing he'd regret it tomorrow. He also knew that wasn't an option anymore.

"I'd give her a compliment," Ian said.

Lust shrugged, bringing his hands up and holding them waist high. "That's what I *just* suggested," and Gluttony waved him off again.

"Such as?"

"I don't know. I'd have to see her before I knew what I'd compliment."

"You wouldn't walk up to her if you were not attracted to her. Pick something generic. Something simple," he said.

Ian leaned against the rail, rubbing his temples with his thumbs and bringing his fingers over his eyebrows to hide his face. He breathed out, "how about *'you're pretty'*?"

Lust drawled out a long expletive as he walked away. Gluttony stayed put. "That's a start. You're comfortable saying that?"

"Yes."

"What's one step beyond that? The thing you're not comfortable saying but is close?"

"Why would I pick something else? I just said I'm..."

"To live in comfort," Gluttony said, "is to die where you were born."

Ian took a deep breath and exhaled sharply in defeat. "You seem like the type to read self-help books."

Gluttony's signature grin was back as he clapped him on the shoulder. "Nothing wrong with wanting to better yourself."

Nothing about this would better him, Ian thought. He looked around more, noticing all the reasons to go home rather than making a move. Fifty-year-old men were nuzzling up to the teenagers serving them, whose dresses were barely kept below their hinds by the curve of their hips. Women with wedding rings were being grabbed on and cat called.

It all filled him with disgust. The ones who were not being groped or harassed seemed to be in groups, and were left alone because it looked like that's what they wanted. Groups of five or six huddled together either at a table or on the dance floor, some visibly shooing away the men who approached. Lust was one of them, just moments before.

"I don't want any of these women," Ian said. "I want to leave."

"We can leave when you have made an effort," Gluttony said.

"An effort to do what?" came a new voice.

Ian turned to see a sharp-featured twenty-something woman in a dark blue dress, purse clasped in both hands in front of her, and Lust at her side. Her brunette hair was pulled back tight to show off her diamond eyes and angular nose. Ian recognized her as one of the women Lust was talking to a few minutes before. She had looked up at them when Lust pointed.

"Sorry, am I interrupting?" she asked, looking back to Lust.

"No, no, perfect time." Lust quickly moved forward, ushering her into their group with a hand on her back. She kept looking at Ian, occasionally glancing down at the floor, but when her eyes lifted they'd always return to his. To ignore Louie, he understood. Louie was handsome, but with his shorter stature and odd clothing, Ian could see how some women might overlook him. Gavin, on the other hand, was inches taller, and 50 pounds heavier; all muscle. And Ian was standing right next to him.

"We were just leaving," Ian said. "Have an early morning."

Lust jumped up again. "After this round of drinks," he said. A tray of drinks arrived and he began passing them out. Four in all. Lust must have ordered them when he was downstairs, but Ian couldn't tell how he knew how many to order.

"Everyone, this is Brooke—"

"Bella," she corrected.

"—Bella, and she was just tellin' me how attractive Ian is."

Ian nearly choked on his drink as Lust finished, Bella still looking right at him.

"It could be a late night, if you stayed," she said.

Her voice was smooth and inviting, like Envy's was, but intentionally sensual. He was considering it for a brief moment, the faint tug of arousal pulling at him, before her hand moved over to his knee. Ian knew who he was. He knew what he looked like. Not an ugly man by any means, but not one a woman walked across the bar to hit on.

He brushed the hand off. "I don't know what he told you, but I'm not interested," Ian said, gesturing to Lust. He was taking a sip from his drink, refusing to meet Ian's eyeline. Gluttony was sitting back, pursed lips and an odd expression he had not seen on the Spirit before.

"He told me you needed some company," Bella said. "Doesn't everyone?"

Ian looked at her, then back at Lust, who still avoided him. Bella's smile never wavered, the invite still lingering between them.

"Lust, a word?" Ian grabbed the man by the arm, pulling him away from the table.

"Oi, paws off. This is Italian—"

"Is that woman a prostitute?" Ian asked when they were far enough away to not be heard.

Lust got a fake look of contemplation on his face. "I don't think they're called that any—"

"You tried to set me up with a *whore?*" Ian seethed, shoving him.

"And I was goin' to pay for her too, you ungrateful twat," Lust spat back.

Ian straightened up, ready to hit him.

Gluttony had stood, quickly moving over to them. "Ian—" he began.

"Stop talking," he said to both of them, and was surprised they listened. "What was the point of tonight? To fuck a woman ten years younger than me? Or to trick me into sleeping with a prostitute?" he asked, glaring at them.

"To give you a confidence boost, boyo. Datin' is about energy, and yours needs a pick-me-up."

Ian ignored the barb. "This place, and the people *in it*," Ian said, eyeing Lust, "are disgusting."

A faint look of hurt pulled at Lust's features. "Do you have a problem with me?" he asked.

"Are you not the reason for all of this?" Ian asked, pointing around the room and thinking of all he had seen in the brief time tonight. This club, and anything like it, would not be where he would find a new wife, not that he even wanted one.

"How many people are out cheating on their spouses tonight because of you? How many women are assaulted *nightly* because of you? *Lust?*" Ian spat the word, not to say his name but the idea itself. Lust was sexual temptation. He was the embodiment of sexual assault, infidelity, and much worse things Ian only thought of now as the anger boiled over.

"Are you not the reason for *cheats* and *pedophiles* and *rapists*? How many children have been molested at the desire you throw on people?" He could not control himself, his voice rising loud enough to gain an audience from those around them, but he didn't care. From over Lust's shoulder Ian could see the young woman was long gone. Good riddance. Lust's face remained vexingly neutral as Ian went on. "You are a plague. The worst this world has to offer."

They stared at each other for a moment that felt like an hour, Ian indifferent to those watching.

"You don't know me," Lust said evenly.

"I'm damn glad for it," Ian said, turning to his ride, Gluttony. "I want to leave."

Gluttony looked back at him, contempt on his face, but Ian didn't care. He didn't bother to look in Lust's direction. There was nothing they could say that would wash him of the dirt and the grime he felt on his soul.

"Let's just go home," he said again under his breath, walking toward the door before either of them could get in the way.

11

He begs and he pleads, softly, to no one in particular. It is audible, though under his breath. It is in his movements and his stillness. Demons of a different breed plague him in the long hours of the night. It is most prevalent in the quiet of the dark, and it robs him of rest. He asks for respite with his very being, and will not receive it. The singular thing we have garnered from our long stint among them is their incessant hope. It is their hope that breaks them in the end.

Sleep evaded Ian the next two nights. He was restless and anxious, awaiting Envy's return from her trip.

Ian had accused her of not having a job and found he was wrong. She traveled to distant places in search of rarities: clothing, rugs, tables, antiquities of all kinds. Some came to the house; others he wasn't sure about. The one thing he knew was she stayed busier than all the others combined.

He wished for her to be back. To have her calming presence return to the house. Ian had stuck to his room for all but meal breaks and the liquor store run he made late Friday night, to avoid Lust and Pride, but also Gluttony, who now blared music from sunup to sundown two doors from his.

Things had remained contentious between Ian and Lust, though Gluttony seemed to have put it all behind them. Any chance the man had, he asked Ian to go for a run or lift weights or to watch him pose. A bodybuilding competition was coming up that he had been training for, which Ian had no desire to know more about. But he awaited Evelyn for another reason, and the wait was over.

Ian climbed the narrow stairs that evening and made his way to the black door at the end of the hall, the only room occupied on the second story. He knocked on the solid wood door, the sound echoing in the corridor behind him. A few beats passed and he heard the creaking of wood slats growing closer before the brass handle turned and the door swung wide.

Envy stood in another understated outfit that would surely get praise from anyone who saw it. A colorful but muted blouse was tucked into skin-tight jeans. She was wearing, of all things, heels. Even though they were just in the house, Ian felt underdressed.

"Do you ever just put on sweatpants?"

"And be mistaken for a commoner?"

She moved to the side of the entryway, gesturing him into the room. Ian gawped at what he saw. The spacious master bedroom felt smaller than it should, with walls lined in finery. Paintings, tapestries, clothing racks, and jewelry stands. A suit of armor was being used to hold clothing either discarded or not yet hung up after a recent shopping spree.

One person could not possibly need all this, Ian thought.

The ceiling came to a sharp point at the far end of the room, just over a large window. The bed sat to the right of it, diagonally in the corner. An unusual setup, but the way Envy had designed the room layout worked, like everything else she did.

Ian thought this room must have been the servants' quarters or the attic in a distant past, large enough for more than one person back

11

then, converted in a renovation. Dark wood paneling covered the walls, floor, and ceiling. A circular iron chandelier hung gracefully from it. It was not the most modern room in the house, but easily the most elegant.

"Do you like it?" Envy asked, seeing the expression on Ian's face.

"I love it," he said earnestly.

"It could use a touch-up. I didn't find anything useful at the trade show," she said. "The floors are a bit squeaky and there's an armoire from Budapest coming to auction next week; it will be perfect over there."

She pointed to the corner opposite the bed where a large wooden chest sat. Ian didn't see the issue with the chest, or why the room needed an armoire. The floors were a bit squeaky, but you could hardly see them with the ornamental rugs scattered throughout.

"I wouldn't change a thing," Ian said, and Envy smiled a smile that didn't reach her eyes.

"Well, spit it out," she said, and Ian gave an involuntary laugh at her bluntness.

"All business with you then?"

"You don't seem the type to seek someone out unless it's for something," she said, as a tinge of guilt flashed across Ian's face. "It's not an accusation. We are here to assist, so if you need help with something, tell me. We don't have to do the dance."

Ian nodded slightly and put his hands in his pockets in an effort not to fiddle with them. "The other day, you…when you showed me that vision…"

Envy continued to look at him with questions in her eyes.

"…I was wondering if you can take them away?"

"You have visions of your own?" she asked in disbelief.

"No, no. Not like what you showed me. It's more of a daydream, I suppose. A nightmare, really," he said, thinking out loud. He found his hands back in front of himself, his thumb rubbing the inside of his palm. "It's just my mind wondering, and I want to know if you can…stop it."

The air hung between them, growing uncomfortable for Ian. He could tell it was also uncomfortable for Envy.

When she finally spoke she asked, "Is this about your suicide? Do you think about trying it again?"

"No," he quickly shot out. "Well, yes, I think about it sometimes, but that's not what this is about."

Ian had to look away from the unbearable relief on Envy's face. He didn't want the weight of whatever lay in her eyes. Whether it was pity or sympathy or fear, this time it made no difference to him. Unable to hold her gaze, he looked at the floor now, where he often found his confidence.

"It's about my wife. My *ex*-wife," he corrected.

"What do you see?" she asked.

Ian wasn't just looking away from her now: his entire body had turned, facing one of the tapestries on the wall depicting a Roman Catholic procession moving through the streets of some unmarked European city. Undoubtedly a priceless object, sitting in this rundown old house.

"I see her…with him," he said.

Envy again didn't reply, prying for more information with the weight of the moment.

Ian obliged, hoping more information might lead to her help. "I found a notebook she had hidden. It had a list in it." He breathed in sharply and uncontrolled. "A library. A park. A restaurant bathroom…. Check marks next to certain ones."

Ian's gaze was fixed on the tapestry, not focused on it but unable to look away. "She was always asking me to be intimate with her in new places. Public places. I wasn't comfortable with it, so I said no. I said we could at home, but when we got there, it always seemed one of us wouldn't be in the mood anymore."

"Check marks...but none of them were you?" she asked.

Ian shook his head, once again looking back to the floor.

To his surprise and further disappointment, all she said was, "No, I can't."

"You can't..." Ian started to ask.

"I can't take that away," Envy said.

Ian didn't know what to say, or do. He had felt so sure of her ability when he came up here, the waking dream of weeks ago so vivid and visceral. He wouldn't have told her all of this had he thought Envy incapable of what he was asking. Of what he needed. The vision she threw him into that first day, she had taken the world off his shoulders for a brief instance. The weight hadn't fallen away, but the new desire he felt pushed it all to the side. That is, until she ended the vision. Whatever that was, he wanted, *needed*, more of it.

The look of defeat hung heavy on his face as he turned to leave the room.

"What I do isn't magic, Ian," Envy said to his back. "Nor is it permanent. I'm recreating what's already there and honing it toward a particular outcome." She had closed the gap between them, forcing him to meet her sight with a tug on his forearm. "Eventually we all have to come back to reality."

"Then why can't you do that with this?" he asked in desperation. "How is this different?"

"You're asking me to take memories from you," she said. "Not even I am that strong."

A heaviness was piling up behind his eyes. *Just make it go away.*

He wouldn't cry here, not in front of her. Not in front of any of them. They already thought so lowly of him. Thought him to be fragile. He shoved it down, focusing on answers. He couldn't keep living like this, seeing the things he saw every time he closed his eyes, the hurt flooding back like the day he had found out.

"Can you give me new ones, then? Something to replace the nightmares."

"I can give you something to want. But it won't make the other things go away, and in many instances, it can make the pain worse."

"*Worse?*" asked Ian. "How can it possibly get worse?"

"I know more than most that manufactured desire will fuel you for a time, give you a goal to chase. But if your chase prolongs, if you don't obtain it, you will turn bitter and…" She trailed off, taking a moment to consider her words. "Well, perhaps if you ever meet Wrath, you'll understand."

The prickling in his eyes had become unbearable. He felt the need to rush out of the room but couldn't bring himself to do it yet. She saw that in his face, gently taking his hand and holding it.

"How do I get it to go away?" he croaked out, but knew the answer before she spoke the word, a soft caress on his hand, a rougher one to his mind.

"Time."

12

It was the faint sound of a TV, maybe a radio. It must be a radio; the only TV in the house was in his room and the sound was coming from the living—

Ian stopped dead.

A gray, human-like creature lay on the floor of the living room with a bucket of popcorn resting on its stomach. Its skin was the same leathery consistency of the creature Pride turned into that day in the kitchen, though their bodies were nothing alike. Where Pride's was slender, sharp angles and jutting points, this one consisted of large rounded features and balled joints. Curled-in shoulders that reached out past its pecs. It lacked a neck. Instead, mountains of muscle formed up from its back, around to the rear of its too small head, which was propped on cushions and watching the fuzzy TV that had been in Ian's room that morning.

The creature turned its head and grunted what sounded like a welcome. Like a hello.

Ian took a step back, bumping into something—someone.

"You took his room, ya know," said Lust.

Ian hadn't heard him enter; hadn't cared to. Ian looked back at the creature, who had turned its attention to the screen once again. Its only movements were the hand that moved from the popcorn tub to its mouth, and blinking.

"His fault, though. We told him to lock his door same as us, that night you got here, but he never listens. Ain't that right, Scooter?" Lust basically yelled on his tiptoes to no avail as the one who was so clearly the Spirit of Sloth returned to his fuzzy program.

Scooter...

"Turns out the only thing he missed was his TV."

"What do you want?" Ian asked Lust. He was the last person Ian wanted to speak with, and they hadn't since that night in the club. It was a very solemn car ride home, with the two Spirits up front and Ian in the back. He felt every bit a child as it looked.

"A real charmer, you are. I can see why the marriage was such a success," Lust fake smiled. "Pearce wants to see you."

"He couldn't come tell me that himself?"

Lust just raised his eyebrows. Of course, Pride would delegate it to someone else, not finding the task worthy enough to complete on his own.

Ian took one last look at the large gray creature on the floor and made his way past Lust without a glance or a word.

"Hold up."

Ian felt a hand grab his bicep so hard his body turned at the force to be eye to eye with Lust. Ian ignored his gaze and looked down at the hand tight on his arm.

"Look, you don't think I have anythin' to offer you, and that's fine. But let me give you a piece of advice from someone who's been around longer than you. We were all in here that first week, whether you saw us or not," Lust said, his eyes narrowing and his voice dim. "Do not think about her when you jerk off."

There was only one woman in the house but somehow, Ian knew, Lust wasn't talking about her. Ian pulled back again in disgust, ripping his arm from Lust's grip. "What is the matter with you?"

"Many things. But take this from me: thinkin' about your wife will

12

only make things worse."

"I didn't ask."

"That's why I offered," Lust said, and flashed a closed smile that reciprocated Ian's joy in this exchange.

Ian's face burned at the thought of them all knowing. He had, that first week. He had used the memory of her many times since the divorce. The only thing stopping Ian from accusing Lust of peeping on him was the admittance it would take to do so.

"First door on the left," Lust said, walking further into the living room to join Sloth on the floor.

Ian turned, storming off to find Pride's room.

⳼

Pride's room was more like Pride's quarters. Taking up the entire left side of the house behind the kitchen, it appeared to have once been multiple rooms now combined with squared archways into open sectionals. A reading space with chairs and a chess table, a desk opposite it, and the bedroom with its four-poster bed off at the end. The quarters were as worn down as any other section of the house, but only in the floors and the walls. The adornments, though aged as well, had an elegance of their own, an aroma of time passed.

Ian had knocked when arriving, not sure from the outside if the room had belonged to Pride or one of the others. He still hadn't learned the full extent of what lay beyond each locked door.

Pride had said, in a raised voice, to enter, and Ian now stood in front of his desk. Pride sat behind it, reading what appeared to be his mail.

Ian looked up while waiting and caught the eye of a portrait of a man from centuries ago. A priceless painting, he was sure. The stone-faced man had a black gown buttoned up to the collar, which was adorned with puffy white material of the time, spreading wide beyond the base of the man's head. Sleeves and cuffs were fitted with the same, though less outlandish, style.

"A handsome face, but I do regret the attire," Pride said, noticing Ian's line of sight. Now he too was staring at the man in the portrait.

"I'm sorry?" Ian asked, confused.

"It was my first body," Pride said, gesturing to the portrait with a silver letter opener. "I have had paintings or photographs done for all of them."

Ian stared in wonder. That was *Pride*? It must have been five hundred years old by the looks of the clothing.

"How many er—bodies have you had?"

Pride didn't answer for a moment, either contemplating or counting, he wasn't sure. Finally turning back to Ian, he said, "More than I've wanted."

As he said it, Ian was once again hit with a wall. They had each lived so many lives, hundreds of years each. At least Pride, Envy, and Lust that he knew of. So many memories; so much history.

"Have you all been together this whole time?" Ian asked.

"Evelyn and I met in the 1700s, though we were not on assignment together at the time. Louie joined in the last century. Others have come and gone over the years..." he drifted, seemingly in thought. "That is not what I brought you here for. You are going to work tomorrow, with Gio."

"So I've been told," Ian said, disappointed how quickly Pride remembered himself.

"You need to be careful," Pride said, offering nothing further.

"You're the one who sent me to him in the first place," Ian said. "Shouldn't you have told me that the first time?"

"I made an incorrect assumption. He does not have your best interests in mind."

"And you do?" Ian asked with disbelief.

"*We*," Pride emphasized, apparently talking about everyone except Greed, "will not only adhere to our directive, but do what is in our power to better your life. Gio has different objectives."

"Then why am I going at all?"

"It is complicated," Pride clipped.

"You've lost track of how many bodies you've had, and there's a five-hundred-year-old picture *of* you, behind you—" Ian's eyes flicked up to it again. "Make it less complicated."

Pride sat thinking for a moment, clearly contemplating not what to say, but whether he should say it at all.

"The—entities—that willed us here are always watching. If one of us has the ability to assist you, and willfully chooses not to, we are punished as one."

There it was. Pride could say all day that he cared. The truth was, if Gio didn't help, Pride's sentence here would be extended, all of their sentences would, and that's all he cared about. Greed wasn't pulling his weight, and they would all be punished for it.

"That doesn't make sense. That would hurt Greed too," Ian said.

"Which would matter, if he cared to leave."

"Evelyn said you and he had a fight after the last person who was in this house."

"We did." Clipped again.

"About what?" Ian asked through gritted teeth.

"That is not of any concern."

"You sit here and tell me he doesn't want to help, that I need to be careful around him. And then you say your fight doesn't have anything to do with that? You all claim you can't tell lies but you do, every time you open your mouths. It may not be outright lies, but it is not the truth—and you know it."

"You cannot discern what you want to know against what you need to know. That is not my obligation to fulfill," Pride said. "You are to be at Gio's office in the morning. Wear a suit."

Pride looked back down at his work, Ian staring at the top of his head, seething.

"And if I don't go?"

"You doom us, and yourself. The only difference is, we have eternity."

"Well, another charming conversation with you." Ian stood, heading for the door. "Next time you want to talk, get off your ass and come find me."

"One more thing," Pride interjected. "As difficult as it may be for you to accept, Louie has much wisdom to share with you. I suggest getting to a place where you can hear it."

Ian exhaled sharply out his nose, shaking his head. Based on what he had seen, he highly doubted that.

☦

A number of the many clothing bags Envy had purchased that now lay in his room contained suits. Blue suits, black suits, tan, and even patterned. An array of collared shirts, but only two pairs of shoes. Black and brown oxfords. Ties to match, which he found to be like riding a bike. Ian used to wear a suit and tie every day. Putting one on now, he felt a slight tug in his chest. A draw and a want.

His instructions were clear, and he followed them to the letter, as he arrived at the same building as his first meeting with Greed. 8.30 a.m., courtesy of bankers' hours, he assumed. This time, when he told the ground floor receptionist his name, he wasn't taken to Gio's office. He was taken downstairs. Ian held out hope that Greed would be wherever they were headed, though he knew as the elevator doors opened to a large windowless basement that that would not be the case.

Overhead panel lighting flowed parallel to the rows of cubicles, the only additions in the sparse gray expanse. Ian couldn't see anyone, could only hear them as they clicked away on keyboards, talked on phones, and rolled their chairs from one side of their cubicles to the other. Before she left, the receptionist guiding him pointed Ian to the slightly elevated corner office overlooking the room like a dungeon master.

Ian knocked and he was greeted by a man who had the same aura as Greed, just less of it. His pinstripe blue shirt and red suspenders were a clash of decor in this gray abandon.

"You the new guy?"

"I think there's a mistake," Ian said. "I was supposed to be meeting with Gr—err, Gio."

"Mr. Costa provided instructions. This way."

They left the corner office, walking along the cubicle rows. Not being able to see over the tops, he received flashes, passing opening after opening of men and women dressed like tax accountants, filling their jacket-backed chairs, row after row. Reading, talking, or typing in the pursuit of some end.

"This one's yours. Trash pickups on Friday. You're allowed personal effects, though they must not exceed the height of your personal area. Over there," he pointed over Ian's head to an open door, secluding a small rectangular room cut into the back corner of the basement, "is the breakroom. Fridge is cleaned out end of the week. No seafood."

Ian took a seat, taking note of the desktop computer, corded phone, and stack of papers on the desk that were apparently for him.

The man pointed to the stack. "That's your first analysis. Any questions?"

Ian started. "Analysis of—what?"

The man laughed, saying as he walked away, "Learn quick, or you won't be here very long."

Ian looked at the stack of papers and was surprised to find, he knew what they were. He had seen similar ones, and studied thousands over the years, while working as a financial advisor. This time, though, they were more detailed. Details that wouldn't have been in public declarations pages.

The stack of papers contained income statements from a business.

Profit and loss sheets outlined by departments and job titles. The name of the company and employee names had been redacted, still showing pertinent information but nothing that would be catastrophic to whatever the business was should these papers get into the hands of the public. The redacted names and additional financial breakdowns here told him this wasn't a publicly traded company. Public information would be—public.

As the realization hit him, a phone rang. His desk phone. Ian half assumed it was meant for someone else and answered hesitantly, "H-hello?"

"If you're going to work here, try to introduce yourself like a professional." Greed. "Did you get your assignment?"

Ian looked at the papers on the desk again, leafing through them. "What am I supposed to be doing with it exactly?"

"You're supposed to understand it."

"In what context?"

"What does Mammon Group do?" Greed asked, a patronizing tone beaming through.

"You're a private equity firm."

"And what do private equity firms do?"

Ian sighed. "They buy businesses."

"So the context would be?"

"You want to know if you should purchase this business."

"Very good. Looks like you don't need me after all."

Ian seized the opportunity. "Actually, I thought the point of this was to learn *from* you." He poked his head up, looking around the lifeless room. "Not to sit in some basement pushing paper."

Silence met him and Ian could feel the disdain through the phone before Greed calmed himself enough to answer.

"First free lesson: having money is glamorous. Making it isn't." He spit the words. "Second: I'm not here to babysit you. I will give you

12

tasks meant to teach, but it is your job to do the work. Third: each day you are here, you will have fifteen minutes of my time. I suggest showing up with questions prepared."

With a click, the line went dead.

Ian spent the rest of the day going over the stacks and stacks of paper for what he called Company X. He couldn't call it anything else, as a name wasn't provided. The documents showed categories of what the business purchased, employee counts, bank statements, shareholder payouts, where income was derived, where losses might occur, and profit margins on a quarterly basis going back ten years. Ian knew the purpose of this task; it was the same thing he did as a financial advisor. To become an expert on all things Company X.

When one company acquired another, they only did so with the intent of making more money than they spent on it. It would take years to claw back the initial investment, so the task was to find out where cuts could be made to speed up that timeline; where the company was over-spending, and what their big money-maker was, so they could invest more in that.

He was aware of the practice, since private equity constantly changed the market. Buying divisions, or even whole companies, stripping them for parts or streamlining profits before reselling. Sales were usually quiet until fully complete, as it would affect the stock prices of the involved parties if the company were public and create a panic if they were not, since the practice usually involved job cuts. Now Ian was on the other side.

It was similar to the old feeling of putting on his suit and tie, though this time, he didn't care who gained or lost.

13

It wasn't long before Ian found a routine. And part of his routine involved locking his door before he went to bed, only to have Gluttony—*Gavin*—come knocking on it at 7 a.m. to go for a run or a weightlifting session. After the first week, he was getting up before his alarm clock went off, just to get ready and leave before Gluttony could find him.

Ian had prepared what he would be wearing the night before, and even looked forward to what he'd uncover in the redacted documents on his desk. The information was a labyrinth he could lose himself in, a puzzle of sorts, trying to work out both what the company did, and who they were. He *had* missed it, he found. Never much of a people person, Ian got into financial advising for the data, not the camaraderie and certainly not the sales. It was what had made him good at his job—before he ruined it all.

Greed was as clipped and disinterested as always, answering Ian's questions with as few words as he could while hardly looking at him. Most of the time, those questions were answered over the phone.

"How do I know where to cut costs, if I don't know what the company is?"

"The most expendable parts of a company are the people."

"How do I know which *people* to cut, if I don't know what they do?"

"One in four jobs at a company are unnecessary. Start with duplicated roles."

His callousness was not surprising given the Spirit he embodied. The surprising part of the routine was when Ian came home. Wanting to do nothing and not wanting to be bothered, he would sit down in front of the TV in the living room, backward on a borrowed dining room chair. He had found the popcorn stash in the cabinets and helped himself to a buttery bucket, surprised it was allowed in the house with Gluttony's strict diet. Ian wasn't sure if it was this or the TV that drove it, but he would inevitably be joined by the one who had moved the TV in the first place.

The day Sloth joined him, it felt eerily similar to being stalked by a tiger. Ian was watching some black and white sitcom from the 1960s and heard a floorboard creak between a delayed laugh track. Ian turned, but no one was there.

He turned back to his show and moments passed with no sound heard. He was almost at ease when he felt a presence, quickly glancing back, and jumped at the oversized gray figure standing against the back wall. Perfectly still, the creature did not meet his eyes, like a child thinking *if I can't see you, you can't see me.*

It was larger than previously thought, his protruding gut the size of a laundry basket and his head well over halfway up the wall toward the twelve-foot ceilings. Ian couldn't tell this the day Sloth was lying down, but the striking size was evident as Ian debated resuming his show or watching his back. After a few moments of perfect stillness, and tracking Sloth's eyes to the TV, Ian decided he was safe.

The next time he checked back, Sloth had lowered himself to the floor, sitting against the wall with his knees up and arms draped across them. Full, Ian put the popcorn bucket under his chair and resumed watching.

Minutes later, he was three feet from the wall.

Then five.

Then ten.

By the end of the episode, Ian could see leathery gray feet out of the corner of his eye and heard the crunching noises of cold popcorn.

They sat like that, in the blissful silence of afternoon reruns until Envy interrupted, apologetically. Even the large brute could not ignore her, as it lifted the nearly empty bucket to her and grunted in offering.

She chuckled her thanks and turned it down before turning to Ian. "How does dinner sound, Friday night?"

"With who?"

"With us," she said. "You and me."

You and me. How many men would kill to hear that from her. He knew she didn't mean it like that, but couldn't stop the thought.

"Sure. What for?"

"To celebrate. One week on the job!" she said with a smile, and left them to it.

Ian turned around to see the giant looking back at the TV, bucket still in hand. This time he could have sworn a frown pulled at its mouth.

☥

"This place is far too nice for me," Ian said as the attendants walked away.

A stewardess had led them to a table covered in fine cloth, twin candles illuminating the small center. Two more white-jacketed attendants waited in the wings, one to take their coats, the other to get their seats. Ian nearly jumped when the man placed a cloth napkin in Ian's lap. He knew which fork to use from various anniversary dinners over the years, but he could pay his own way back then.

"Nonsense. It seems like things are going well at work. I hear you were even up before Pearce this morning. You're adapting quickly."

"Being busy helps with…everything," he said, thinking back to the conversation in her room. Ian was still embarrassed at his admittance that night, realizing she was the first person to see him cry since his wife nearly two years prior.

Envy nodded as he said this, quiet contemplation on her lips.

"I'm glad you have that outlet," she said, holding up the wine list. "It only helps for so long."

He knew he shouldn't ask, already knowing the answer. "Is there something else you think I should be focusing on?" he inquired as the waiter arrived, cutting off their conversation.

"Anything catch your eye, ma'am?" he asked.

Evelyn smiled back. "The 88 Mouton," she said with a lilt, handing off the menu.

Ian waited for her reply at his still lingering question. She pretended to think, giving space for the waiter to leave, and Ian knew immediately he should have followed his gut.

"Gavin says you're still ignoring his advances—"

"Please don't call them that."

"And you'll have a hard time finding someone to court if things stay stagnant with Louie," she continued.

"You've been talking to Pearce," Ian said with thinly veiled disappointment. "I thought this was a celebration."

"It is. And he is wiser than he looks," she said.

"Which one?" Ian mocked and Envy eyed him to cut it out.

"He's a walking cock," Ian said. "The actual embodiment of sleaziness. It's in the name *Lust*. I have nothing to learn from him."

"So you have nothing to learn from me either?" Envy asked.

"It's not the same—"

"It is," Envy said. "You view him as a demon in every sense, you wear it on your sleeve. Aside from Pearce, he seems to be the only other one you do. You can't pick and choose. Either we are all evil, or none of us are."

The waiter returned as Envy finished her scolding, pouring wine. Ian leaned back as they waited, fiddling with his lap cloth.

And waited.

"Everything to your liking?" the man asked, looking at Envy, who was trying the aged glass and not even acknowledging him.

Ian wanted to throttle him, at both the clear moment he was interrupting and the pointed flirting with his date. It wasn't a real date, but he didn't know that.

Envy smiled as if nothing was wrong. *"C'est parfait,"* she said. Of course she spoke French.

In Ian's experience, upscale restaurant attendees often looked at the man to order, though Ian noticed he was asked surprisingly few questions, compared to Evelyn, when their food order was taken, and was not even glanced at as the waiter left.

He was steps from the table when Ian started anew. "What Lust stands for is an abomination to society. Pearce is ego, you are desire. Gluttony is a steroid junkie, best I can tell. Harmless qualities to people other than yourselves. Lust is a plague that ruins lives."

"*Louie* represents an easily identifiable fault. I promise you, our brethren in spirit of pride, gluttony, *and envy* have caused far more issues in history than you care to know. And for the record, those are all names designated by humans," Envy said, glancing around as they grew louder.

"What do you mean by that?" Ian asked, taking the bait.

Evelyn's attention returned to him. "Lust, Pride, Envy…these are not our names. They are what your kind have chosen to call us. Labels for the worst of our capacity that overlook the root of our ability. We are not evil; we just have the capacity to be. Are humans so different?" she asked rhetorically but Ian knew immediately they were not.

It grew quiet between them, and Ian took to looking around the intimate yet expansive room. They were on the younger side of the guests, mostly gray-haired WASPs, carrying an air of superiority in their fine pressed suits and pearls. Money floated in the room like air, natural and unworried, juxtaposed with the stiff conversation it accompanied. Greed would have loved it.

They didn't speak again until the food arrived, the silence of forks and knives unbearable any longer.

"He tried to set me up with a hooker, Env—Evelyn."

"He should have told you about that, but regardless, do not look down upon them."

"With all due respect, they're selling their bodies for cash. Not exactly future senators," Ian said.

"Is that so wrong?" Evelyn asked genuinely.

"It's…" Ian thought, unable to put words to the feeling of discomfort rising in him. "It cheapens it," he finally said.

That night in the club, he hadn't felt so disgusted since the day he discovered his wife cheating. Sleeping with a prostitute wasn't cheating if he was already divorced, and it was consensual, but regardless. A rebuttal rose in him at the mere thought of it.

"Do you think me cheap?" she asked.

"What—" Ian started. "No, of course not. You're nothing like her."

"I was, once," she said, taking a bite off her plate. She stared at him, not coldly or assuming, but waiting. When he did not speak, she continued. "We weren't handed anything when we came here. We all had to make our own way, contributing how we could. There weren't many ways back then for a woman with no connections—no history at all," she corrected herself, "to make a living. I could scrape together coppers and food working as a barmaid. But any substantial money was to be found upstairs, behind closed doors. And I took it. For a better life."

Evelyn finished and looked down at Ian's half-full plate. "You should eat more. You're too skinny as is."

His appetite had abandoned him, a cold feeling lingering in its place, and he quickly searched for a new topic.

"Why do you live in that house if you're all so rich?" Ian asked, more put off than he'd like to admit at how her wealth and what was being spent on him was earned.

"We made the switch some hundred years ago. A group of strangers moving to a new city, living together in a fanciful mansion, received too much attention. Better to make home in a place that's not so...boastful, but we need the size. Additionally, it helped our subjects," Evelyn said, peering up at him through her eyebrows. "Your life is supposed to get better from here. Not worse. To go from living lavishly to a one-bedroom apartment never did well for their outlook."

"What exactly am I to learn from him? What is his core, then?" Ian asked, returning to the topic of Lust. It had lingered between them and would continue to do so until resolved.

"He told you, the first day you met. Do you not remember?" she asked.

Ian thought back to that day in the kitchen, seemingly months ago now but only a few weeks in actuality. When he thought he was being attacked by intruders. Pearce had introduced himself as Dignity. Evelyn as Desire, and Lust...

"Passion," Ian said with a sigh. Envy was quiet. He could feel she wanted to ask something, and when it finally came out, he understood why.

"Can you tell me you had passion in your marriage before you lost her?"

A knife entered his chest. It only missed his heart as it sank to his gut, increasing the hollowness there.

"I loved her, and I'm not the one who left."

"Did she feel that, or just hear it?"

He went silent again, heat rising in his face. He hated that he got like this when things got hard, but his other option was yelling, fighting to prove he was right. None of them knew; none of them were there day in and day out. What could they tell him of his own life that he did

13

not already know? How could someone know more than him if they had not experienced it? Just like the therapist. What did those on the outside know of living on the inside?

Silence returned to them and they sat in it until the check came. He'd never felt like such a child in all his life, fighting with a parent who now paid for his meal.

"I'll pay you back," he said as she reached for the check. He hated how it sounded rolling off his lips.

"I do not want money. I don't need it," she said.

"Made enough, then?" he asked, implication clear in his voice, layer after layer of emptiness nesting in his gut at the remembrance of her past. He regretted the words as soon as they left his lips.

"No," she said, her words lacking the spite of his, making him feel all that more devoid. "I want a favor."

He knew that day in the mall, the moment he accepted anything from any of them, it was not charity. It was a debt. Ian exhaled sharply. "What kind?"

"Make peace with Louie. And listen to his advice."

They did not speak on the trip back to the house, and Ian's mood had not only lingered, but worsened. He was a pawn in their schemes. Constantly manipulated, pushed and prodded in directions he did not choose. He told Envy she was not like the others—but that was a lie. She was exactly like them. Putting him in debt to control his actions. He wanted to yell, to scream, to have it out and tell her every horrible thing he thought about each one of them. He could not bring himself to do it, though. His fists clenched and his knee bounced, needing to move, to do something. To be anything but still.

It was hardly a thought, more of a reaction, when he entered the house and went directly for the last remaining room he had yet to enter. With all the others occupied, it had to be the one.

The blaring music that could always be heard pulled him to the room like a siren call. Two quick knocks was all it took before the door flung open, a wide smile greeting him.

"Look who it is."

"Tomorrow morning," Ian said, and Gluttony's expression grew wild. It would have frightened him if he was thinking clearly.

☦

When the alarm went off, Ian regretted it. The anger and frustration, while distantly present, had dissipated and all he wanted to do was sleep.

He slapped the snooze button moments before Gluttony burst into his room shouting, "Gooood morning VIETNAM!"

Even having agreed to the workout, Ian realized he should have locked his door. It was too loud, too abrupt, too…much. Gluttony was sporting his signature attire from that night in the kitchen, with the addition of gray sweats to fend off the morning chill.

"Get out," Ian mumbled, rolling over. He could hear the too quick footsteps making their way toward him.

"Now what kind of workout partner would I be if I let you quit before we even started?"

"It's too early," he mumbled, dozing off quickly.

"You can get up on your own or you can deal with the consequences," Gluttony said to his back.

Ian was too tired to think of what the consequences could be, and was just about asleep when his mattress moved from under him, throwing Ian sideways in a rumple of blankets and pillows to the hardwood floor. Jolted awake, he peered up to see the too muscular man leaning on the mattress he had just tilted like a seesaw.

Gluttony let it fall to the floor, convinced his job was done, and headed to leave. "You have five minutes."

Envy, to Ian's chagrin, had anticipated this day, and he found some of the clothes she had previously purchased to include gym attire, though not as well fitting as the others she had bought. Shorts that rode a little too high and a shirt that clung a little too tight around the midsection, accenting the gut that had somehow persisted while the rest of him frailed.

Gluttony was back in the room minutes later, holding out a water bottle with pink liquid. "Drink it."

Ian smelled it, a faint aroma of artificially flavored pink lemonade wafting up. "What is it?"

"Go juice," Gluttony said, and Ian eyed him suspiciously. "Some pre-workout, BCAAs, and creatine," he finally said. "Nothing to worry about."

While Ian drank that, Gluttony circled him like the hairdresser from the mall.

"What do you want to focus on?" he asked, looking Ian up and down.

Ian had never really considered this before. He had never worked out in his life. Gym class in high school was probably the last time he had attempted to run a mile, but never weightlifting. Ian kind of assumed if you worked out, it all got better. His physique wasn't too far off from his high-school days, just slimmer in all the parts where muscle should be and thicker in the middle.

"The area below my neck," he said, blinking the morning away.

Though Gluttony owned a car, they ran to the gym some twenty blocks from the house. He said Ian 'could use the extra help'. The 'go juice' did help, but Ian ran numbly quiet while Gluttony was entirely too energetic for the sun to have recently crested the horizon.

The gym in question was an open-air facility that probably once served as a mechanic's garage or storage service. Large bay doors opened on both ends to allow a breeze, with thick rubber mats lining the floor. It was more packed than he would've assumed at this hour, with middle-aged men and women twenty years older than him, both in significantly better shape.

By the time they arrived, Ian was doubled over grabbing his knees.

"You asked for this," Gluttony grinned.

"I had been drinking at the time," Ian panted. He only had one glass of wine, but still.

"Yes, well, I lost Wren as my workout partner, and you're not her, but I need a new one, so hurry up and catch your breath." Gluttony was stretching in ways Ian wasn't sure his body could contort, going from yoga poses he recognized, to others he had never seen before.

"Wren?"

Gluttony's face indicated he didn't understand the question before straightening out. "You would call her Wrath. The workouts were unbelievable," he said dreamily.

Ian looked around, making sure they weren't overheard. Others were focused on their workouts, headphones in and absent. "Wrath is a *woman?*"

Gluttony laughed. "Of course. You've never heard 'hell hath no fury like a woman scorned'?"

"But..." Ian racked his brain. It wasn't so much an influx of words in thought, rather feeling. Pictures and moments he associated with his own gender. "Wars, genocide, murder...isn't most of that done by men?"

"Maybe, but Wrath isn't the reason for that. That's ego. Pride. Men wishing to impose their will on the world. Women usually use more... finesse," he said, moving over to the bench press, Ian following.

"What happened to her?"

"She's in...timeout," Gluttony said, getting under the bench press. He had put two large black plates on either side. Ian squinted and saw the number "45" on each one and his heart sped up. "Which means I lost the greatest workout partner in seven realms and *you* have large shoes to fill. Spot me."

They rotated positions for nearly an hour, Ian watching carefully so as not to harm himself, and hardly being able to do ten percent of Gluttony's weight and movements. He wasn't sure how spotting would help. If the weight fell on Gluttony, there was nothing Ian could do to stop it taking off his head.

When Ian finally had a second to keep pressing, Gluttony cut him off. "No one in the house talks about what happened with Wrath. Not really our story to tell."

"That's the same thing Envy said about the fight with Pride and Greed," Ian prodded. "Did it involve Wrath as well?"

Gluttony made a face indicating he had said something he shouldn't and tried to change the subject. "You should focus on those of us trying to help you and ignore the ones not here."

"So Wrath fucked up and I'm down one of the seven dwarves?" Ian joked. Despite the pain in his chest, arms, and legs, Ian found he was in a surprisingly good mood, which dissipated as Gluttony dropped any semblance of his warm, inviting demeanor.

"That is *not* what happened," he said, "and do not ask me about her again."

Ian found it unsettling how often he truly forgot they were Spirits. He talked of them constantly—knew at surface level they were not human. But it was times like this, when their eyes hardened and their tones shifted, that it fully hit him. They were demons. They could call themselves Spirits and helpers, but they were here on a prison sentence for deeds he still didn't fully understand. Sentences hundreds of years old. He briefly wondered what one could even do to deserve something so harsh, and searched for a question that would ease the tension again.

"Why aren't you fat?" he asked. He had basically asked it the night they met, and received a laugh. Ian thought he knew the answer, given the unnatural physique, but more than anything he hoped it would garner the same response as last time.

"Used to be," Gluttony grunted between sets. "Then I discovered tren."

"Tren?"

"Trenbolone. Steroids," he said, side-eyeing Ian and still lifting. "You want some?"

"Err—should you really be trying to give me drugs?"

"They never did me any harm."

Ian stared at him deadpan. "You're immortal."

"And you're going to die eventually. Why not look good in the meantime?"

Ian closed his eyes, exhaling. He was only now realizing how little the Spirits thought of mortal life. Everything they did were the actions of people who could do and undo a thousand more. Take new bodies, change old faces, move, abandon and relocate away from any mayhem they might cause.

"Though I think it causes much of your kind to lose their hair. Can you pull off bald?" Gluttony asked. He squinted and held up a thumb between himself and Ian, presumably blocking off Ian's hairline from his line of sight to get a visual. After a moment he dropped the hand and pursed his lips. "On second thought, never mind."

As the workout ended, Ian realized he'd barely be able to walk back, let alone run, which he could tell Gluttony was about to do. He also knew enough about working out to know he'd be in worse shape tomorrow.

"How exactly is this supposed to help my situation?" he asked. He felt the burn in every joint, muscle, and fiber of his body and wondered why he'd ever agreed to come.

"Evelyn says you've been having trouble sleeping."

"And?"

Gluttony just smiled that too perfect smile; one that said he knew more than he let on.

13

"And ask me again tomorrow," he said.

Ian had a hard time believing that would matter if his legs gave out before he could make it to the house.

14

Ian couldn't believe it as he opened the gate to Dr. Bardot's backyard, waddling through, his legs hardly usable two days from his workout with Gluttony. So much had happened in the month since their last meeting. So much had changed, and yet so much had stayed the same. Life progressed, but it could not go unnoticed that he still felt nearly identical to the last time he had stepped through these gates.

The doctor disagreed.

"You seem to be progressing," Bardot said, already starting her scribbling.

"What makes you say that?" he asked.

"General demeanor seems to be improving, and you don't appear as sleep-deprived. What changes have you implemented?"

At least that part was true. He'd never give Gluttony the credit, but the early-morning workouts all but ensured he slept through the night by the time he could crawl back to bed.

"Started lifting weights," Ian said, reaching up to scratch behind his ear self-consciously.

More scribbling. "Exercise has a number of benefits, including the release of endorphins and improving sleep quality."

Ian had to will himself not to roll his eyes. "So I've been told."

Bardot didn't skip a beat. "By who?" she asked.

Ian remembered he hadn't mentioned the Spirits in the first session.

He was going to, right before he was interrupted by Pride in his head. Ian found he had a small smirk on his lips, recalling how he once thought he was going insane. It flattened out when he supposed he still could be.

"I have...roommates." Not entirely false. It only now dawned on him that she would not be privy to all the information of his living situation. She had recommended him for the program, but was not an administrator over the process, and he was positive she was unaware of who lived there.

"Do you get along?" she asked.

"Some are better than others," he said noncommittally, and she waited for more information. He sighed, remembering their deal. "One is very nice, two are tolerable, and the other two are...not what I would have chosen."

"That's quite a lot of people," she said almost challengingly.

"It's a big house."

She scribbled some more. "Tell me how they affect you. Specifically the two you do not get along with."

What could he tell her that would make any semblance of sense? That they were demons who manipulated him. Who claimed they could not lie or harm and yet seemed to skirt the fringes of that when it suited them. That they were serving prison sentences hundreds of years long and had the audacity to question his decision-making. That was something.

"They are in similar positions to me. They're not in the house by their choice, and we...talk. About what went wrong. Normally about my life more than theirs," he said. "With very little information, they talk to me like they know more about what happened with my wife than I do. As if they were there. As if they would have handled everything differently and it would never have happened, which is incredibly hypocritical considering they're in the same shoes I am."

"And how does that make you feel?"

"Really?" Ian asked in a droll, annoyed tone.

"It may be a cliche line, but it's asked for a reason. Would you prefer I assumed?" she asked.

Ian refrained from telling her that she did, often.

"It makes me feel…that I'm the only one who has fucked up. They don't ask me questions. They make statements. They tell me what happened and why, as if I wasn't even there. Do you know what that's like?"

He stared at her, waiting for an answer that never came. "To be made to feel you made all the wrong choices. That everyone around you would have done it better? And they don't know that they would have. They just want you to know that they wouldn't have ended up like you." He finished and her scribbling continued well after he stopped speaking.

"You accused me of something similar once. Do you remember?"

"Yes. You were guilty of it too," he admitted this time.

"I apologize. I didn't mean to make you feel that way, nor do I now. But I must ask, if no one can attempt to offer insight into your life without receiving an admonishment, how do you intend to learn?"

Ian didn't answer, knowing where this was headed.

"I don't mean to imply that everyone should get an open invitation to give you advice, but you must find someone who you trust and heed what they say."

"I do," he said. "I trust you."

She seemed surprised by this. "Do you?" she asked.

"More now than I did," he shrugged. It was true. He found it easier to talk to her. Still more guarded than he'd like to be. But even one month ago he wouldn't have openly admitted as much as he had in the past thirty seconds.

"What about the one in the house who's nice, who you get along with.

Do you trust them?" she asked. This would have been significantly easier to answer two days ago. Ian hadn't yet let go of everything from their dinner. Talks with Envy were wonderful, most of the time. He felt conversation flowed with her more easily than it had with anyone in years. And yet.

"I'm not sure. She can be manipulative," he said.

"Do you think it's to your detriment?"

"Does that matter? Manipulation is manipulation."

"Some people take the wrong route to get to the correct destination. Perhaps trust isn't the right word," she said, breaking to take further notes. "Do you believe she wants what is best for you?"

"Yes." Another truth. An easy one. Even if Envy was acting in her own self-interest, he believed her interests and his were aligned, unlike Gio. Gio's goals were entirely different from his own, but at least Ian knew that. He didn't trust Gio, and what he felt for Evelyn was polar opposite to the Spirit of Greed.

"May I ask, what does she tell you to do?"

"She tells me to trust the others."

More notes. "Hmm, a crossroads then," she said.

"A crossroads?" Ian asked.

"Well, I suppose the question would have to be asked: Do you trust her more than you distrust the others?"

He wasn't sure how to answer that. Pride hid from him too much and the others helped keep his secrets. Lust seemed to lay most of it out on the table, chaotic as it was, and it's not that he distrusted Lust so much as he wondered about his competence. And then there was Gluttony. Ian only recently discovered Gluttony even existed; far too soon to make a judgment call.

When Ian was unable to give an answer, Dr. Bardot moved on. They covered how his sleep had increased, the bags having left his eyes. If he thought more about self-harm, which hadn't changed much since their last meeting, and he caught her up on his new employment. She was thrilled with that.

"It appears you do trust me. I seem to remember advising you to find something similar to your old work. I'm glad it paid off."

Though she wasn't entirely able to claim that success, he let her have it. It was easier than telling her the Spirit of Greed owned a private equity firm and was ordered by a higher power to give Ian employment.

"However, if you have resumed employment, we will no longer be able to provide financial assistance. The home, of course, is still yours for the remainder of the period but the deposits will cease. I'm sure you understand."

Ian nodded. He knew this would happen eventually but had hoped it wouldn't be for a while longer.

"One more thing—" She held up the familiar medical cup and cap as the session came to an end.

Ian had stopped taking the meds for the most part, but began again two days ago to ensure they were in his system. The grogginess and lack of energy was noticeably reintroduced to his days, getting hardly anything done since then. It wasn't the end of the world, he thought, as he took the cup into the restroom and closed the door. Two months down, four to go.

15

"Where were you yesterday?"

The moment Ian sat at his desk, his phone rang, Greed on the other end. Ian rubbed his eyes, not yet ready for the day.

"With my therapist," Ian said, not sure Greed even needed to know.

"What's the point of being alive if you need another human to dictate how to be one?"

Ian sighed, not in the mood to deal with this. "It's a contingency of the program I'm—"

"Meet me outside," Greed said, and hung up before Ian could ask where 'outside' meant.

Minutes later, he stood on the rain-slicked sidewalk in his plain black suit and white button-down. Mammon Group occupied one of the busier blocks of downtown, making it difficult to focus between the layers of mist and passersby as Ian tried to spot Gio. His hair was soaked through by the time he heard a shout.

"Sir!" someone yelled, and Ian turned toward the voice, toward the street.

An elderly man in a blue lapel and black gloves stood in expectation, hand on the door of the most expensive car Ian had ever seen. The man opened the rear door, holding an umbrella over the top.

"Let us get you out of the rain," he said congenially.

Ian stared back between the car and the man, confused to the point of immobility, only broken when Gio peeked his head around the corner. "Get in before you ruin my seats."

Ian moved then, crouching down into the opposite side, the door closing behind him. It was a different car than Gio brought to the house weeks ago, but Ian assumed it was one of many the mogul owned. The interior was a cream-colored executive layout, with two rows of spacious seats facing each other. His boss had his back to the driver, Ian facing him.

"Do you not own an umbrella?" Gio asked, grimacing up and down at his dripping hair and rain-spotted coat.

"Do you ever just say hello?" Ian asked. The car had begun moving. "Where are we going?"

Gio had looked down at an open folder in his lap. "We're buying it," he said.

"Buying what?" Ian asked and Gio finally peered up, the look of bored contempt always present in his eyes.

"The business you have been evaluating," Greed responded, and returned to his folder.

Ian lit up, feeling his shoulders rise. It felt like the first time he made a profit on a stock purchase. All the hours mulling over the data, thinking through the economic impact on what could change in the next three to five years. Running through scenario after scenario and coming to a conclusion that felt like finding a coin you had dropped in a field months prior. He had done what he was supposed to and it felt good. Good enough for a smile to creep to his lips before he was quickly drawn back to reality.

Greed didn't like him, and wouldn't do anything he didn't deem absolutely necessary. "Why bring me?" he asked.

"Because the entire point of this exercise is to teach, and even though I could do without you there, it will be a teachable moment nonetheless."

They didn't speak again until arriving outside a two-story building on the outskirts of downtown, located in a recently gentrified part of the city. Once underpriced warehousing, it now consisted of overvalued office space and desirably rustic living. The sign out front glowed in amber light: *HMS: Health Management Services.*

Another car waited out front, which Gio explained was his legal team for Mammon Group.

As they climbed out of their own, Gio stopped him. "Don't open your mouth in there. I don't care if you're having a heart attack or need to sneeze, you keep quiet until it's over and let the lawyers work this out. Understood?"

In any other circumstance, Ian would never allow anyone to talk to him like that, but he had to admit, he wanted to see what it was like. What it felt like to watch his hard work materialize in such a way. An entire business was being purchased, and it was all his doing. Ian nodded in agreement.

Inside, they were ushered to a glass-paneled conference room overlooking the open-concept work floor. Rows and rows of brand new desks, computers, and chairs, occupied by a young staff mostly in jeans and T-shirts. Three people waited for them, all in suits.

"Tom Ryan, Head of In-House Counsel." He reached over the table and shook hands with Gio's lawyers as Ian and Gio sat. "And my colleagues, Diane and Manuel," he said, gesturing to the others on his side.

Gio also had a team of three lawyers, though only one introduced herself: Janel.

For the next two hours, the six of them combed through a stack of papers brought by each side. The sale price was agreed to long before they arrived, but they bickered relentlessly over clauses and addendums outlining the terms of the sale, and the assets being purchased.

In the cluster of legal terms, Ian was able to work out that Health Management Services was a late-stage startup. They had built proprietary management software specializing in healthcare, with a sizable client base of independent hospitals, which made more sense now that Ian could correlate the data he'd been combing over against the truths he now learned.

At the end of the session, all documents were signed and, apparently, in effect.

The opposing lead counsel, Tom, stood. "Congratulations: You are now the proud owner of HMS," he said with a large and genuine smile.

Ian couldn't help but feel pride well in himself at his participation. "I look forward to working together."

Tom extended his hand to Gio.

Gio kept his hands down, resting on the table. The woman to his right, Janel, spoke instead. "Mammon Group thanks you for your services, but they are no longer required."

Tom's face fell in an instant, his hand half lingering in the space between. "Are you firing me?" he asked slowly.

She shook her head. "Laying off the team," she replied, gesturing to his colleagues, "Our legal department is fully staffed. An unfortunate necessity of acquisitions, as I'm sure you understand," she added with a smile, though her eyes conveyed anything but empathy.

In the moments that followed, Tom's team went through various stages of grief as the remaining employees looked on from the outside. Threatening legal action, pleading for answers, and finally growing quiet in the acceptance.

Ian did everything he could not to lash out himself. He held his tongue until the three released employees were escorted out.

"What the *fuck* was that?" Ian seethed.

Gio looked at Ian as if he were a child. "I need to speak with Janel. I'll meet you at the office," he said before exiting with his lead counsel and leaving Ian in the conference room.

Ian returned to the chauffeur, who was waiting right where they had left him, umbrella in hand. In the car ride back, and the elevator ride to the penthouse floor, Ian's anger solidified. He had beat Gio back, and the secretary wouldn't let him in the office until Gio arrived.

When he did, he walked right past Ian, sitting in the plush leather singles.

Ian followed. "Why do that on the spot? You humiliated them on purpose," Ian said, the doors closing them in. The room had changed little since his last time there. His first time, actually. Ian's daily fifteen minutes with the man were held via phone calls, and the rare occasions Greed visited the basement, though rarely with the intent of seeing him.

"I did what I told you I was going to do—teach you," Gio said. "You put together a convincing report, but you weren't aggressive enough in your suggested cuts or layoffs. You still don't understand the reality of this. This isn't a charity or a welfare office or a daycare for overpaid interns. We exist for one purpose only. Profit. If a job is not needed, it is cut. If a salary is too high, it is cut. So you know what we get in return?" Gio asked, his cold eyes harder than stone.

"An overpriced car?" Ian spat.

"Sustainability," Greed said, his glare softening slightly. "Companies hire to meet the needs of the future, which offers two possibilities. They either obtain the future they desired, or they fall short. Today, HMS achieved what they desired. They were purchased by a private equity company and their founders will ride off into the sunset, never having to work again. Everyone else will either be repurposed for a new future, or let go. When a house has been built, Ian, it no longer needs the builders."

Gio went to his desk, opened a drawer and pulled an envelope out. Flat, white, and thin. Room for a single check.

"I brought you today because you are good at this. Your report was the best of anyone on your floor; detailed, thorough in its possibility, but you didn't suggest a single layoff or budgetary cut. You could have a real future in this business, but you need to leave the bleeding heart behind. You didn't have one when you bought and sold stocks of companies doing the exact same thing; why have one now?" he said as he slid the envelope across to Ian.

He had no idea how much something like this was worth. Probably not a lot, considering Gio had just spent tens of millions on the acquisition and wouldn't be keen to increase that number, but it was something. Ian didn't respond to the Spirit as he thought through the proposition.

Greed was right. Publicly traded companies had a cycle he knew all too well, and profited off of regularly. They would expand, build a new division, new software, a new factory, and then announce layoffs while citing the need to 'restructure'. An announcement that always meant one thing: higher profit margins, which meant a higher stock price. It was no different than what they just did, only now, he had to see the faces of those affected.

"What happens now?" Ian asked.

Greed smiled. "We do it again."

He deflated further. "That's it? Just on to the next?"

"If you wanted a parade, you're in the wrong business."

Ian steeled himself. It was a rare time indeed, and regardless of Gio's consistent quips, he was in a noticeably more patient mood than Ian was used to. He looked to take advantage of it.

"A parade seems a bit much, but I do have a question."

Greed did not respond, simply raising his eyebrows.

"Were you friends with Wren?" Ian asked into the silence. He used her human name on purpose, rather than the Spirit she embodied. Pride once said Greed didn't like to be called anything but Gio. He wondered if it would be the same for Wrath. He also half expected the same shouldered response he received when asking the others about her. To his surprise, Gio extended his grin.

"You'll want to avoid the basement, if you don't want to end up like the last one."

"The last one? The last person to live in the house?" Ian paled.

Greed's grin changed to a smile of a cat playing with a mouse. "No, nothing to worry about. I suppose everyone's learned their lesson."

He went back to shuffling papers around on his desk, pretending the conversation was over. Ian knew, though. If it was over, Gio would have kicked him out.

"This is my life you all are playing with. I deserve to know."

"Well then, ask him." Pride. It always came back to Pride.

"He won't answer and you know it. All the others will say is it's not their story to tell. They say it was between you and him."

"It was." And then, after a second, "it is."

"And? Do you owe him so much as to keep his secrets?"

"Far more than I owe you," Greed said, his face rigid once more. After a moment, he began to contemplate, the grin playing on his lips at the game before him.

Greed reached into another desk drawer and slid a large, thick manila parcel across the desk, looking to contain more paperwork. Ian's next assignment, no doubt.

"Get this back to me by month's end, with something I can use, and I'll tell you whatever you want to know."

"I don't suppose you'll tell me more about this one than you did the last?" Ian asked.

"Actually, you'll know less about this one. It's a larger acquisition. A parent company and its subsidiaries. We risk too much as it is. If anything leaks, that basement will be the least of your worries."

"Great," Ian said drolly, although excitement lit inside him. He'd have it back within the month, and he'd find out exactly what he wanted to know.

16

Every time he stood outside one of their doors, Ian felt it. The reminder that this was not his home, that he was a guest. Behind every door was something or someone he was not privy to by right. And he hated that feeling. Of not standing there waiting on a friend, but to ask another favor. He hated it more knowing it was Pride he had to ask.

Ian entered the quarters to find them exactly as he had left them the last time. Old furniture and paintings with an aroma to match. Pearce sat behind his desk, as per usual, and Ian wondered where he went all that time he didn't spend at the house.

Pride didn't look up as Ian approached and said, "I need a ride."

"Ask Gavin."

"At the gym."

"Evelyn?"

"New York."

"Louie?"

Ian pinched the bridge of his nose, trying not to lose his temper while he needed a favor. "He doesn't own a car and you know that. Why are you even in here all the time? What could you possibly be working on?"

Pride finally looked up. "You'd have to ask Evelyn that. What's wrong with the tram?"

More secrets. Last time he inquired about Pride, she had shut him down. At least this time, Ian had permission. "Nothing, other than it would take over three hours to get there and back with all the public stops. It would take a fraction of that if you'd do it."

"Right," Pride said with an exhale and set down what he was working on. "Very well. Where are we going?"

"To the bank." Ian held up his first paycheck. It was somehow more and less than he had expected, and also wondered if it was entirely legal that he had worked an entire month and received only one check. Having closed a multimillion-dollar acquisition, he thought he'd be paid at least ten thousand, but thinking about it further, he figured it seemed on par with the way Gio ran things. Which was to say, greedily.

They left the house minutes later to companionable, though tense silence. It was always tense around Pride, in the rare occasions he was even there. Like saying or doing the wrong thing would get someone in trouble. Maybe it was the way Louie and Evelyn looked to him, or the air he naturally carried, but Ian ruefully sat in the feeling when Pride broke the quiet.

"I have an inquiry."

Ian was looking out of the window, focused on getting there and being done with this excursion. "You're giving me a ride; not sure I can say no." It was still again for a moment, just long enough for Ian to face Pride with curiosity.

"You attempt to end your life. It does not work, and then you wake to all of—this," Pride said.

"That's not a question."

"Why are you still fighting?"

"What does that mean?" Ian asked. His tone held more hostility than he probably felt, though he had no idea what Pride actually wanted to know. He didn't feel like they were fighting until just now.

"There are certain things I do not understand about humanity. After all this time, one would think us experts," he said. "You live such short

125

lives, yet still choose to advance their end."

"Oh," was all Ian could muster.

"It is not a suggestion that you should or should not; merely curiosity," Pride said, more flustered than Ian had ever seen him. "I do not see the connection from where your life was, in an attempt to take your life, to where it is now. In all honesty, I half expected you to try again in those first few nights."

"You act more human than you'd like to admit," Ian said, taking in the way Pride gripped the steering wheel. Something about it made Ian grin. He truly was worried. Or perhaps Pride was just flustered at his inability to control a situation. Ian wondered if they were all this worried. At what lay in the balance should he actually go through with another attempt. Seven Spirits doomed here for who knew how much longer. They had all been here for hundreds of years, as far as Ian knew, and he had little to give, but he could give reassurance.

"I—" Ian began, and paused to think, realizing he had never thought about it before. About why. He thought back to the days and weeks leading up to that decision that didn't feel like a decision at all.

"I didn't want to die. I don't think anyone who takes their own life wants to die. I think they're just tired."

"I must admit I still do not understand," said Pride.

"When I tried—when I did what I did, I was out of ideas. Out of options. Or at least it felt that way. But mostly, I was out of the energy to keep trying. When I woke in the hospital, I wasn't 'fixed,' he said, "but I felt slightly rested, and though I wouldn't have admitted it at the time, I was mostly relieved that it didn't work. I felt ten percent better. And you can't quit when you've got something left. I knew then, as I know now, that as long as I have ten percent, I have energy to fight. It may go away again. The pain is still there. I still want it to end. But as long as that's there, I have to try."

"Does it remain at ten percent now?" Pride asked, and Ian was happy to know it did not. That it was higher.

"No," he said. "I'm not sure where it is now, but I know I want to try, at least, to make things better."

He wasn't prepared to give any of them the credit for it, considering he was still on the outs with Lust, hadn't even met Wrath, and Pride, though helpful today, had hardly done anything other than give orders and make his presence sparse.

Pride nodded in acknowledgment before asking, "Is Gio assisting with that?"

"And to think we were having a semi-good moment there."

Pride had begun to slow down and Ian could see the building they were headed to. "You do not know what he is capable of."

"I don't know what *any* of you are capable of," Ian shot.

Pride grew quiet as he put the car in park.

"What does a *spirit of the underworld* have to do to get a five-hundred-year prison sentence? Murder a whole village? Create a plague? Rain hellfire on the peasants?" Ian mocked. "And mind you, he's not the one locked in a basement, so he can't be that bad."

Pride didn't answer, only stared ahead, his hands planted on the steering wheel. Knowing the conversation at an end, Ian got out of the car and went inside, leaving Pride to wait.

He waited in line till he made his way to the front, then was met by a wave, gesturing him over. He took a seat at the clerk's desk.

"How may I assist you today?" the woman asked.

Ian set his documents down on the desk, along with his first check from Mammon Group. "I need to open a checking account."

The clerk took his documents, entering information into her terminal. Ian took the time to look around the bank interior. He had never liked banks. While everyone else complained about the DMV, Ian had complained about banks. They felt like the DMV, just with a risk of being in a robbery. A bland cinder-block interior, lined with middle management offices and water coolers. People in off-the-rack suits waking daily to process check after check, deposit after deposit in an endless cycle. His windowless basement job seemed less depressing.

"Oh, dear," the woman said, looking at the computer screen. Her eyes were wide with surprise.

Ian sat up straighter, heat rising to his hands and face. "What?" he asked.

"Sir, I apologize, but we won't be able to assist you today."

Ian just leaned forward, confusion on his face. She turned her screen to him. On it was a list of data he didn't recognize. He saw the headline ChexSystems, with a number in a small outlined box.

"203."

"What is that?" Ian asked.

"This is your ChexSystems score. It's different from a credit score. This is a rating of your history with past banks, as we're all connected through the federal system," the woman said. Her face held a look of pity that still confused him.

Ian looked at the number again then back at her. "That's high, isn't it?" he asked, hopeful.

She shook her head slowly. "It maxes out at 899."

Ian deflated, sitting back in his seat, arms slumped over the sides. "What am I supposed to do if I can't open a bank account?" he asked.

"It will rise over time, but unfortunately with this score, we won't be able to open an account with you as the primary holder. If you had someone to list as a co-owner..." she trailed off as Ian sunk deep into his chair, closing his eyes. He exhaled deeply at the dread creeping in, knowing what he had to do.

⸸

The window was rolled down on the passenger side door when Ian arrived back at the car.

"Can you come inside." It was more of a statement than a question.

16

Pride looked at him with a blank expression. "What for?"

"I need—" Ian started and stopped as Pride's smile grew. The smug bastard knew Ian was about to ask for help, and was going to gloat. Ian wouldn't give him the satisfaction. Ian opened the car door and climbed back in, his check still in hand. Pride looked down at it.

"Never mind."

"I am not an expert on human matters, though I am aware you are supposed to leave that inside," he said, the smile still on his lips.

"I can't. They won't give me a bank account," Ian said, returning the smile with a fake one.

"And why is that?" Pride asked.

"Because, the last one I had, I abandoned with a highly negative balance."

"A pity," Pride said, hands thrumming the steering wheel, looking into the distance.

Ian bit his cheek to stop his reply. He'd find another way to get an account. Wait until Evelyn was back, or talk Gavin into it during their next session.

"So, ask then," Pride said, pulling Ian back to his dilemma.

"I did ask, they told me—" Ian started, only to be cut off.

"*Ask* me," Pride insisted.

The smile had left his face, though Ian felt he was being talked to like a child.

"You wouldn't help me even if I did," Ian said. He didn't know that for a fact actually, but didn't want to give in. He already owed Envy; he would not put himself in the same position with Pride. He didn't trust this was out of the goodness of the Spirit; it never was.

"You have a very short memory, and are far less cunning than I had hoped," said Pride.

"I swear to god, if you insult me one more—"

"What did we tell you that first day?" Pride asked.

Ian ignored the question, taking in a sharp breath. "Do you ever let people finish their sentences?"

Pride contemplated this as if it weren't asked rhetorically. Ian rolled his eyes when he realized he was actually going to receive an answer to the question.

"Yes," said Pride. "When they are saying something worth hearing. Now, what did we tell you on day one?"

When Ian didn't respond, Pride continued, *"If given the opportunity to assist, and we choose not to, we stand to be punished further,"* he said as if reciting from a rule book.

Ian wasn't sure what clicked, but it no longer seemed he was asking for help. Asking for help put him at the mercy of those he didn't want to owe, in either spirit or material. With this new-found information, it seemed instead he was demanding assistance and somehow that was easier to do.

"I need you to cosign on my bank account," Ian said.

Pride leaned in with a fresh smile on his face. "Why didn't you say that sooner?" he asked.

Ten minutes later, Pride was filling out his own set of paperwork with the apologetic bank clerk.

"Oh, and Ian?" Pride said.

Ian looked over to the man aligning himself financially to a bankrupt vagabond.

"If you abuse this in any way, I will kill you and deal with the consequences later."

The woman behind the desk did a poor job of pretending she didn't hear that, but Ian left the bank with a brand new checking account and a credit card to boot, happy that one difficult task was done. One to go.

17

Ian paced, exhaling sharply through his nose three or four times trying to muster up the courage. One of the few rooms in the house he had yet to enter, afraid he might leave with something he didn't bring with him.

"I can hear you out there, boyo!" Lust called through the door, a cheer in his voice.

Ian muttered a curse and opened the door slowly, cautiously eyeing through the widening crack to make sure he wouldn't catch a glimpse of anything he couldn't unsee.

He was surprised to find the room was actually rather—clean. Perfectly clean, he realized. Brighter than he would have imagined. For weeks he pictured a dimly lit sex dungeon with swings and velvet and candles. He could not have been more wrong. The bed was covered in white linens, a teak floating headboard behind it, an area rug perfectly squared in front. The walls were a muted white over the aged wood, save for a singular dark accent wall that shelved his books. Before it, Lust sat in one of two expensive-looking chairs, reading. In his signature tracksuit, Lust looked more a tourist than an occupant.

The only other thing remotely suspicious was the mirror on the ceiling.

"You read?" Ian asked from reflex rather than spite.

"A' course," Lust said, setting the book down on the footstool before him. "Keeps me wits about me."

Ian tried to peer at the cover. Unable to read the title from across the room, he could only make out what appeared to be a Roman statue on a solid black background.

Something must have shown on Ian's face. The hesitancy.

Lust sat up, constrained excitement dancing on his own. "Is this it? Are we havin' the sex talk?"

"I'm thirty-two years old and was married for a decade. I know what sex is."

"You know what it is, but if you knew how to do it proper, she'd a never left you."

Ian turned to go. "This was a mistake."

"No, no, no. Stay. I'll behave, I promise."

He had a look of pleading on his face, uncharacteristic of his usual self, that made Ian stay. As much as he did not want to have this talk, he had known something was off. They had all agreed on it. Including Evelyn. Dr. Bardot's question made him realize he did trust her more than he distrusted Lust and Pride, he just wished he could skip this part.

"Why do you want to help me so badly? And before you say it's because you have to, I know this goes beyond that for you," Ian said.

Lust acted like Ian had brought up his first love; awe spread across his face.

"Being intimate with someone is the second best thing in the world. Ya know what the first is?"

Ian shook his head reluctantly.

"Helpin' a friend get laid," Lust said with a Cheshire Cat grin.

"We're not friends."

"We could be if you weren't so tight in the rear."

"You tried to have me sleep with a prostitute, which for the record feels like a lie—"

17

"I never said she wasn't. You assumed she wasn't," Lust corrected.

"—the point is, I don't trust you," he said. "But Evelyn does. And she says I should give this another shot. Which I will, but only if you agree not to lead me into anything that you willfully know I won't want to do."

Lust contemplated this for a second, clearly trying to find a loophole in it. Ian wasn't sure if he found one or not when Lust said, "I'll agree to that. If you apologize."

He didn't have to ask what for. That night in the club, he had said worse things to Lust than he had ever said to anyone. Worse than what he yelled at his ex the night she left him. The night he found that black book. He still felt that way, though. Lust was the embodiment of everything he described. The cause of it all. He wasn't sure how to move past that. The Spirits might not be able to lie, but he could.

"I'm sorry for what I said. I didn't mean it," Ian said, and apparently it worked.

Lust smiled and nodded, rubbing his hands together. "Where do we start?"

Ian took the seat opposite him. "I...suspect," he hesitated, "that I may need pointers....with women."

Lust's face lit up as Ian finished, though still trying to hide his excitement.

"Right, right," Lust nodded. "I've seen enough to know that."

Ian glared at him.

"Sorry," he said, raising his hands again. "I just mean, you seem the type to second guess yourself. Women can sense that like there's a sign over your head."

"But what do I do about that?"

"Well, there's a few ways I can help. First off, we can have a threesome. I'll guide—"

"You can't possibly believe I'm going to agree to that," Ian sighed,

133

dragging his hand over his face.

"I didn't, but all a man can do is ask," said Lust. "If that's out, I guess we'll just have to walk through the details."

"Look, in spite of the other night, I know how to talk to women. When I want to. I'm more concerned with what to do when, you know…"

"When you're starin' at the pink cave?" Lust asked, as equally straight-faced as Ian stared back at him, neither giving an inch.

Ian couldn't tell if Lust was trying to rile him up or if this was genuinely how he thought human beings talked. He wasn't sure how long Lust had been on Earth, but it was enough to learn how to be a jackass.

"It's a dance, love. Most women want to be led. They want you to do what you want to do—within reason," he stopped, eyeing Ian. "You're not into anythin' weird, are you? It's fine if you are, but you gotta ask a lady before you go prodding in places you shouldn't."

"*No*, Jesus, I—"

"I'm not gonna tell you again. Stop sayin' that. Now," said Lust, "This is the dance—you should want to make her feel pleasure, but you should also do what feels natural to you. If you're all stiff or hesitant, they're gonna sense that, lad. The only thing worse than that is being a selfish lover. Don't ever be selfish." He slapped Ian on the cheek.

Ian jumped back in shock. "What was that for?"

"A reminder," Lust said, and Ian tried to focus on the mission at hand over the still-present desire to leave or hit him back.

"It's the same when datin', actually," Lust continued. "You say you know how to talk to women? Well, that means you have to know when to talk and when to pipe down. You feel where the conversation's goin', so you know when to ask questions and when to listen. Sex is just like that, but with your body."

"What—what do you mean *do what you want but don't be selfish?*"

17

"I mean, if you want her on top, put her on top. If you want her from behind, climb on her," Lust said, gesturing aggressively with his whole body. "That passion you feel—she will feel it. But while you're doing that, feel her too. She'll talk to you with her body the same way you talk to her with yours. Got it?"

"No," Ian said, and Lust gave him a look of incredulity.

"How do you usually fuck?" Lust asked.

"Can we not call it that?"

"See, that's your problem right there. You seem to have an issue even discussin' it. Why is that?" Lust asked, and it appeared to be, for the first time, a genuine question from him rather than the usual quips.

Ian knew the answer, and equally knew Lust would not understand. In Ian's experience, those who spoke so casually of sex acted casually about sex.

"We see things differently. Can we just accept that and focus?" he asked, and Lust resigned with raised hands.

"How do you usually *make love*," he exaggerated.

Ian raised his own hands. "Normal? I don't fucking know. What does that even mean?"

"Do you have a routine? A move? How long does it take?"

"I don't know. I guess, and maybe…fifteen minutes?"

Lust looked back at him with the same pained expression. "You're givin' me nothing here. What am I to do with guesses and unknowns? I'm not in your bloody bedroom. But I could be…?" Lust waited to no avail before continuing. "Our house has thin walls. You've heard me do things the Father below has never dreamed of. Stop being coy and paint me a picture."

To his dismay, Lust was right. He had seen things and heard things he never wanted to from Lust. But Ian found the vulgarity and openness of the relationship made it easier to explain, tastefully as opposed to Lust's crude nature, what he normally did with his ex-wife. Giving in, he told Lust how it started, the usual move he did, and now that he thought about it, the move he had used every single time for ten years, and how long it normally lasted. He gestured the motions with his hands and when he was done, Lust's face was a mixture of awe and skepticism.

"And she likes that?" he finally asked.

"*I don't fucking know. That's why I'm here,*" Ian seethed.

"Have you not an intuitive bone in your body?"

"There's a sex joke in there somewhere," Ian said, face flushed and finding himself trying to shift the focus from his growing ever hotter skin.

Lust was thinking, which made Ian even more uncomfortable.

"Alright, apology not accepted," Lust said, standing up and leaving Ian on the couch.

"*What?* What's that supposed to mean?"

"It means I'm not over it yet," he said, playing hurt but amusement in his tone. "I will be after you apologize."

"I did apologize—"

"Not with your words, boyo. With your *actions,*" Lust said, and grinned from ear to ear just as Ian's phone buzzed.

He let it go to voicemail and excused himself from Lust to hear his mom's voice.

"Ian, let me make this very clear. We are getting the family together to celebrate Dean's graduation. You're expected to be there. If you are not, we will be showing up wherever you are. And yes, I'm aware we don't know where that is, but I'm your mother, and I'll find it."

⸷

"This is ridiculous. And cruel. For her more than me," Ian was saying, though he certainly didn't want to go either. Lust was holding sweaters in front of Ian trying to see which he liked more. "How'd you even get her to say yes?"

17

Lust took a break from styling Ian and looked at him as if he had asked the stupidest question known to mankind. Ian and Lust were on better terms after the other night, but Lust still insisted the apology was not just owed to him, but to Bella, the prostitute from nearly a month prior. He had somehow convinced her to go on a date with Ian, which he now supposed involved an exchange of money. The odd thing was, Ian wasn't to plan anything. That was taken care of, Lust said, which for some reason irked Ian now that he had his own money to spend.

Three hours later, Ian was sitting on a bench next to the river when she arrived.

She walked up and smiled at him sheepishly. More than he deserved, he supposed.

"Hi," he said.

"Hello."

They stood at a distance, unfamiliar territory between them.

"You look very nice."

She did too. The blue dress from that night in the club was replaced by a sleek black one. Her hair was down this time, outlining her face in curtains to her shoulders; flats rather than heels. She didn't look like a prostitute. He wasn't sure what even signified that.

"You do too. Very handsome," she smiled.

She was probably just saying that, but he did like the outfit. Lust had picked out a short-sleeve white oxford with a sleeveless knitted sweater to go on top. His hair was roughly combed back and the scruff had grown out enough that he no longer looked like a man child.

"About the other night—" he started.

"Don't worry about it," she cut him off, shaking her head. "Let's just focus on tonight."

He could do that, he supposed. It had been a long time since he had been out with anyone who wasn't a demonic spirit forced into his life, and despite her profession, she was very good-looking.

"Louie said the evening is planned. What did he tell you this time?" he asked.

She bit her lip with a grin, clearly wondering how forward to be. He didn't blame her, after their last encounter.

"He says I shouldn't sleep with you. In fact he paid me not to." She chuckled as Ian turned beet red. "He says you…do things out of necessity, rather than enjoyment. He says you play things too safe, and that I'm supposed to get you out of your comfort zone."

"He's an observant little bastard, I'll give him that." Ian laughed and found it was actually genuine. "I'm certainly out of my comfort zone now. No offense."

He eyed her warily. They had begun their walk closer to downtown, not knowing where they were headed but following her lead. He was having a good time, though he wasn't prepared to pretend it wasn't still odd for him.

"None taken, and me being here isn't what I have planned for that." She smiled mischievously as they continued their walk into the city. "What did he tell *you* about tonight?" she asked.

"He said not to call you a prostitute again," Ian joked through pursed lips.

To his surprise, she gave a laugh of her own behind a hand-covered mouth.

"Not to be insensitive, but what is the proper term?"

"Don't suppose there is one, really. They're always changing the name. Trying to find something that doesn't have such a negative connotation."

"Do you think it's working?" Ian asked.

"I think you have to admit 'escort' sounds better than 'whore,'" she said.

Ian turned beet red again, blurting, "I'm sorry. I shouldn't have ever—

"

"It's okay," she said, cutting him off again. "I didn't know you didn't know what I was. Probably would have handled it better on my end as well," she smiled. "For the record though, I prefer 'Bella'."

"Bella," he repeated. "I can do that."

They continued walking until reaching a warehouse. It was properly lit but with no signage, the kind used for event rentals over long-term use. They entered to a cashier station, where they bought two different kinds of tickets, Ian happy to put his debit card to use for once. One participant and one observer. Ian had a feeling he wasn't going to be the observer but tried his best to stay composed in light of all he owed. He owed a good night to Lust. To Bella, for how he acted last time. To himself in the wake of it all. He could be a good sport for one evening.

They walked into what appeared to be a makeshift science classroom. Rows of rectangular metal tables seating two at a time, lining the room up to the front, where a larger single table lay. Blankets, pillows, and small bottles on it. Standing next to the table was an attractive woman in her mid-forties, curled sandy blonde hair, and what appeared to be a red nightgown.

"Nude painting?" Ian asked. That wouldn't be that bad. He had taken an art course in college and, although he'd never had any live models, wasn't opposed to the idea of sensual art.

"Mmm. Not quite," Bella said.

They were ushered to their table in the back right of the room. Most of those surrounding them were men, but the occasional woman could be found in a grouping. On their table was a box of latex gloves, and nothing else, giving Ian an uneasy feeling in his gut.

Soon after taking their seats, two assistants moved from the back of the room. One began handing out information packets, while the other, a man in semi-formal attire consisting of slacks, a button-down, and a tie, addressed the room.

"Thank you all for joining us. We will begin in a moment. You will be called up in order of your table numbers. Please remember not to do anything that you are not strictly told to do. Veering from the instructions will result in being escorted off the premises. Take a moment to review the information in front of you. We hope you have a pleasant experience."

Ian flipped through the material. It was a medical packet that included a vaginal diagram, and descriptions and instructions on the female orgasm. He was still wrapping his head around how it could possibly be useful in that moment, when the woman in the robe stepped forward.

"Hello, everyone. I am Veronica, and welcome to this session of Orgasmic Meditation—"

The woman kept speaking but Ian tuned her out, looking down at the box of latex gloves and over to Bella.

"No," he said.

"Yes."

"With you?" he asked, fast and hushed. She may have been an escort but she also mentioned Lust had paid her *not* to do anything sexual.

Her eyes shifted over to the robed woman. "With *her*."

A man from the crowd had cheered at something Veronica said and snickers came from around the other tables. Ian's attention was pulled back to the front as Veronica disrobed, fully nude, and climbed onto the table with her legs up, her side facing the crowd. The two men from the front left-most table had put their gloves on and were making their way to her. Veronica seemed to already be giving out instructions in a conversational tone meant only for the two men in front of her at the time.

"I'm not doing this." Ian stood up to go. This was worse than being with a prostitute. Not only was he paying for it, he was going to be watched by others? He could hear Bella's seat move from behind him, following him out past the cashier and onto the sidewalk.

"Wait!" she called, but he had already stopped. He didn't know where he was going, he just knew he had to leave the building.

"Whose idea was this?" he asked, spinning around.

"It was mutual."

"You know I'm uncomfortable with this," Ian said, gesturing to her to imply her profession, heat rising to his face, "And yet this is the idea you come up with. How is this any better?"

"It's a middle ground."

"Between *what*?"

"Between you not being willing to talk to strangers to meet someone new, and not willing to pay for it from a professional," she said, raising her hands in frustration. "Something has to give."

"Why is it such a problem that I don't want to sleep with some random stranger?" he asked.

"It's not about that," she said, "It's about moving on. Emotionally."

Ian's face contorted. "What's that supposed to mean?"

"You know what it means."

"What did he tell you?"

"He didn't just tell me not to sleep with you, he told me everything," she said, trying to tread carefully but losing patience.

"He said your wife is the only person you've ever been with, and that's beautiful. I mean that. I'm sure when you married her, you thought she'd be the last one you ever slept with," she continued, "But she's not living by that anymore, and neither should you. And, for the record, this isn't sex." She gestured to the warehouse they stood before. "It's a demonstration. You are not betraying her by being here. You are not devaluing what you had with her, or what you do with others in the future."

It felt like that, though. It felt like doing anything with anyone meant he could never go back. More than that, what did it say about who he was? One year ago he had been married, he had a great job. A great family. Friends. He was respected in their community. Now he was a single man, broke, and standing with a prostitute in front of some warehouse for a sex demonstration.

He shook his head, exhaling deeply through his nose. "What am I supposed to tell the next woman I want to be with?" he asked. "That I...I was so fucked up I had to pay to touch a woman?"

She grabbed his hand. Not a romantic gesture but a comforting one. "You tell her that you had been through hell and back and you did what you had to, to get through it."

He looked back up at the warehouse. "This is how you think that happens?"

"This is just supposed to be fun," she said, smiling. Not just smiling but beaming. Considering what she was talking about, it was so odd it was endearing. "It's meant to be a little weird. You think everyone in there isn't put off by it? That's why it's done in groups. There's safety in a shared experience."

She had a hand on his arm now, practically tugging on his sleeve, and he felt himself loosening up. She leapt on it.

"Veronica's a friend, and a professional. The participants are not allowed to touch themselves; it's not a peep show, it's to learn and have fun. Each table only gets about five minutes. Five minutes and it'll be over and we can go do whatever you want."

Against his better judgment, he knew she had won. He was prepared to say yes ten seconds ago and she saw it in his face. He looked around, stalling for time.

"Okay, but then I pick what we do," he repeated, and she nodded, hiding a grin, before they went inside.

Bella was right. It was a shared experience. One by one, tables would go up and be told something or other from Veronica, who spoke while looking down at herself and gesturing occasionally. Once the men got the hang of it, she'd lean back and enjoy it, somehow ignoring the murmurs from the observers.

It was evident who was doing well and who was not. Veronica was not a silent patient, and made her pleasure known. Equally, a few of the groups were unable to receive such a response and in turn there was much talking between them and her, making Ian nervous. Too nervous. He supposed the only thing worse than going up was going up and being bad at it. He put on a pair of gloves when they were three tables away, only to sweat a puddle into them and put a new pair on. Bella rested her hand on his leg under the table, which for some reason only made things worse.

At last he was called on. As an observer, Bella stayed in her seat. Most of the other men had chosen to keep their backs to the crowd, for probably more than one reason, and Ian followed suit.

Veronica could see the terror on his face and smiled at it.

"Relax," she said. "I'll walk you through everything." She took up his entire vision, her nude body and sensual demeanor forcing everything else to his peripheral. Her head was on a pillow but twisted over to him as he stood over her like a doctor with a patient. "Start with that." She nodded to a bottle of lubricant on the table.

"I'm going to be very direct," she said in an equally straightforward tone. "I'll tell you how to begin and when to move to the next phase. From there, do what feels natural. *You may only touch my vagina with your hands.*"

He nodded at this to confirm.

"When I give additional direction it will be clipped, such as *faster, slower, higher,* etcetera. Do you know where the hood and labia are?"

He nodded again. He had always known where the clitoris was but if he was honest with himself, had never memorized the names of the other parts. The diagram helped.

"With your left hand, put two fingers on either side of the hood, rubbing the labia."

He did so from the top down, angling his elbow toward her face. She was warm against his skin. Too warm. He knew his hands must be frigid to her and felt bad for it.

"Slower and more pressure," she said, either not noticing or pretending not to care. He did so and she went quiet, but her legs opened wider after a short while. He took that as a good sign. "With the same hand, bridge your fingers together at the tip and slowly rub over the clitoris, down to the opening."

As he did so, she rocked her hips up into his hand and he met her with more pressure, leaning into the table to balance himself. A faint moan escaped her and he felt his own arousal growing.

Up until now it had been very mechanical. There was hardly this kind of foreplay with his wife in years past. Sex became a thing they did because they knew they should and he had known for some time it was more for his benefit than hers.

Veronica began to pull back, letting him wind down the motion. "Keep your left fingertips over the hood, and with your right hand, put one finger in the vaginal opening." He grew nervous once more, unable to determine why but looped his right arm under her raised thigh, doing as told. He kept his finger straight as he pulsed in and out at a slow rate.

"Another finger."

He did so, repeating the in and out motion.

"Curl them toward you as you pull them back," she said, eyes trained on him.

He followed her instruction, his fingers now rubbing against a slightly firmer patch of skin. He messed up a few times, finding the dual motions confusing, almost like trying to pat your head while rubbing your belly. After a few attempts he found the rhythm of both hands down and he felt her arch, moaning at the same time. He looked over to her face and saw she had her eyes closed, clutching her breasts. Ian felt like a school kid and couldn't help but grin. He looked back at Bella to see her with the same expression as him before he fell out of rhythm.

"Focus," Veronica said.

He turned back. "Sorry."

He picked the rhythm back up and it wasn't long before she said, "Faster." Her hips rocked into his hands and he tried to meet the pace of her motions as she picked up momentum, "faster."

He listened, trying to maintain equal speed in both hands. His forearms started to burn and he was met with an old familiar sense of pride—the desire to please her more than to give in to the growing ache. He pushed through, rubbing his left hand over the clitoris, pumping and pulling his fingers up and out, brushing the tips against the roof of her opening. It felt repetitive to him but as her body arched and the moans grew more frequent he felt her legs tighten around his hands, her knees pinning together until—

She reached down abruptly, knocking his hands away gently but forcefully, her legs shaking. He pulled back, startled, wondering if he had done something wrong but when he looked up to her face, she was smiling, rosy around the cheeks.

"Good job," she breathed. "You can head back to your seat."

⸸

Bella was looking at him expectantly, a smile from ear to ear as they walked downtown. He could see it from the corner of his eye, not looking her way. Not wanting to give in.

"I'll admit you were right if you stop staring at me like that," he said.

"I thought men liked it when pretty women looked at them."

"They do, but not when they're gloating."

They were walking hand in hand now, which he felt a little odd about considering where his had been, but she didn't seem to mind. He had worn gloves at least and the night had felt more platonic than anything.

"So you admit it was enjoyable?" she asked.

He rolled his eyes. "*Yes*, it was enjoyable."

"Enjoyable enough to do it again?" Her teasing tone turned back to the night they met. Sensual. Inviting. He stopped and turned to her, more aware than ever of her hand in his. "I thought Louie paid for you *not* to sleep with me."

"He paid for my time, which ended twenty minutes ago."

He thought about it. For more than he had in over a year, he gave thought to being with someone other than his wife, and wasn't repulsed by the idea. It was progress. She was beautiful and kind, caring and funny. He could have done worse.

"Thank you," he said, "but I'd sort of like to do something else tonight."

There was clear disappointment in her face but she didn't press. "Such as?"

"I'd like to apologize."

"Ian, you don't—"

"You said I got to pick what happens next. Please," he said.

Her face softened in acceptance and it was a punch to the gut to know he had hurt yet another person. Ian looked down at the ground. He knew he could say what he was about to, and he'd mean it, but had to make sure he got it out.

"I shouldn't have had to get to know you to not treat you as less than a person. I wasn't comfortable with the idea of sex for money. I'm still not, but that doesn't make what I did right," he said.

His gaze remained on the pavement, unable to keep up with the pressure that mounted. "You agreed to come out tonight knowing I was against it and did everything in your power to help with a problem I wasn't even fully aware of. That's more than most people have done for me. I want to say thank you for that, and I'm sorry it took me being an ass to get here," he finished.

When he looked up, her eyes were glossy and her lips were pursed.

He took a deep breath, ready to make another apology for making her cry, when she leaned up on her toes and kissed his cheek.

"Thank you," she said softly.

He didn't know what to say, so he nodded.

She looked at an imaginary watch on her wrist. "I think there's still time to do the other."

He grabbed her hand again, laughing. "Maybe next time," he said, thankful for the ability to let go for an evening. Bella made him feel similar to how Evelyn did—skeptical, but free, and it was a welcome reprieve.

They continued their walk, Bella settling her head onto his shoulder. It wasn't long before she broke the silence.

"How do you know him?"

"Hmm?"

"Louie," she said, looking over to him. "I get the impression you two aren't the closest of friends."

"Oh, right. Well—" Ian fumbled over his words. "We're not friends, not really. We're in a program together."

"Like AA?"

"Something like that," he clipped.

Bella would have known he wasn't in AA, given they were drinking the night they met. She caught on and nodded, letting it drop. There was something about it that pulled at Ian, guilt settling in his abdomen. He was putting a wall between them after all she had helped him let go of, and he hated the sight of it.

"He's just…he's not exactly what I look for in a friend. We don't see eye to eye on many things."

To his surprise, Bella laughed in a way that sounded too much like a scoff. "I would kill for a friend like him."

"For a friend that…buys you an escort?" Ian asked with a humorous lilt to his tone, squeezing her hand, though he wasn't sure what she meant.

"For a friend that cares as much as he does," Bella said. "You should hear the way he talks about you. Even when we met in the bar, he never once talked about himself. Just went on and on about what a good guy you are, and that I shouldn't break your heart. When he called about tonight, I thought he was having a laugh. But after he explained the situation with your wife, he said he just wanted to give you a night that you deserved." Bella stopped to chuckle. "He also said he'd do it himself but he didn't think you would appreciate it."

"That sounds like him," Ian said, surprised to find himself grinning.

Bella squeezed his hand back. "It's not my business, but you could do worse," she said, and Ian had a feeling she was right.

18

Gluttony was in the middle of squatting just over 400 pounds, if Ian's math was correct. Four metal plates on either side of the bar spread across Gavin's back, which caused it to bend just enough to make Ian nervous. He racked the bar, slapped it and looked at Ian. "Your turn."

Ian stared at him and the joke he had told too many times.

"It wouldn't kill you to at least try and lift it," Gavin said, defeated. He knew how this would end and had begun unloading the plates down to a more manageable amount.

"It actually would, and if I survived, I wouldn't be able to walk for a week," said Ian. He stepped under the bar, lifting the meager amount to begin his set.

"Perfectly fine. Can't work out next week anyways," Gavin said.

Ian nearly toppled over. Gavin had never taken a week off from working out. With the gym being one of his few outlets for his true nature, Ian didn't know that was even possible.

He racked the weight again. "You are?"

"Yeah, for the—" Gavin stopped. He was looking at Ian with a blank expression, all thought behind his eyes disappearing in an instant and returning just as quickly.

"Is something wrong?" Ian asked.

Gavin had snapped back to himself but was treading water Ian didn't recognize. "I have to help…someone. With…something."

Ian stared at him, confused. After a moment he asked, "Is this a drug thing?"

Anytime Ian had bought an illegal substance, it came with the same connotation Gavin now presented. That didn't make sense, though; he'd been quite open about his use of steroids in the past.

"No, sorry," Gavin said, before changing the subject. "Have you talked to Evelyn lately?"

Ian allowed the switch, assuming the sudden change in demeanor was a Spirit thing.

He hadn't talked to Evelyn. They'd seen each other in passing, but ever since the dinner, they seemed to avoid each other equally. Or perhaps it seemed like that from Ian's point of view, with as much as she traveled. Envy was abroad again attempting to obtain a new dining table, though Ian didn't understand why. They had never used the one currently in place.

"You all gossip like school children," Ian said.

Gluttony raised his hands, back to himself. "No one's told me anything. Doesn't take a genius to put two and two together."

"And what two pieces are you putting together?"

"First time we worked out just so happens to be after an evening out with her? Whatever was said between you two was enough for you to knock on my door at near midnight," he said.

Ian clicked his tongue. "Fair enough."

"She's back, you know. Got home late last night if you wanted to—"

"Stay out of it," Ian said.

He had been meaning to talk to her since the phone call from his parents—the last thing he needed was his family showing up at the house—but he had stopped himself from going to her quarters multiple times. He didn't want their first conversation to be him asking for a favor.

Since then, he had come to believe if he owed her an apology, she certainly owed him one too. Ian knew he could have handled the information about her past better, similar to Bella. But Envy had not only insulted his marriage, she also manipulated him in the process, though fighting with her hurt more than he cared to admit. Evelyn was the only one in the house who felt like a true friend, most of the time. Now he thought it doubtful he would ever get his apology, but he needed something, and if they were going to use him, he could do the same.

Showered and changed after the workout, Ian made his way up the narrow staircase back to her room and knocked. She probably knew it was him; he had never heard anyone else in the house ask permission to enter a room.

"Come in," he heard through the door.

She didn't bother to turn around when he entered, busy reorganizing shelves with various knick-knacks that looked expensive. It had been over a month since he stood in this room and so much had changed. The armoire she mentioned purchasing during his first visit lay snug in the very corner she had envisioned it. Every piece on the clothing rack had been replaced, and the floor, although still covered in rugs, seemed to be a new color. He also could have sworn the bed frame was new but couldn't remember the previous one enough to know definitively.

"Been busy?" he asked in light conversation.

"No more than usual," she said.

"It looks good," he said, remembering how she lit up the first time he said so. "What do you do with all the old stuff?" he asked. He was trying to make small talk but was genuinely curious. At the rate she changed decor, it was alarming.

"My warehouse, downtown," she said, her back still to him. "You never know when you'll need a spare."

A spare what? Lord knows how many things she had purchased and stored over the years. In his brief time here, Ian had already seen two dining room tables, three mirrors, a chandelier, and whatever had been stripped from her very room. But last time they talked of her wealth, it didn't go well.

"I made up with Louie," he blurted, not knowing what else to add.

"That's nice."

She really was going to drag this out. Anger flared in him. She had started it and couldn't even meet him halfway? Ian tamped it down, remembering why he was there.

"You were right. He is smarter than he looks."

She didn't reply to that, dusting away at shelves that didn't need it.

"And I wanted to apologize."

Envy turned to him, finally, expectation and want on her face, waiting to hear more.

"I said some things. I think we both did," he added.

Her face tightened. "It's fine," she said.

"It's not. I don't know what that's like, to have to make that decision. You made the choice that anyone would, and I'm sorry." This much was true, though he felt it less than his sheepish tone implied, and a half smile cracked her wanting expression.

"Thank you. It was a long time ago. Not sure why it bothered me so, but you're sweet for saying it," she said.

"I also had a favor to ask," he said.

She turned her back to him once more, but he continued. "My parents called the other day. They've called a lot, actually. I've been screening them, not knowing what to tell them."

"Oh? What about."

"They asked me to come over this week, to catch up. I can't keep putting them off but I don't want to go alone."

"Oh?" she asked again, and he could tell she wanted to know.

"I've kind of hidden…everything from them. They know about the divorce and me losing my job, but not much else."

That he lost his driver's license, his financial licenses, the attempt on his life, where he was living. That he was broke.

"My brother will be there too. With his wife, and my nieces. He just graduated with his master's so it's a bit of a celebration and…I feel if I bring someone new, it would keep them from asking too many questions about this last year," he finished.

Though the offer was clearly hanging in the air, she didn't bite on it. The waiting stretched as she resumed her fake dusting.

He had an idea. "I could ask Bella, if you're not up to it?"

She whirled, trying too late to make it look relaxed. "Who's Bella?"

Ian stifled a grin. He didn't want to take Bella, actually. He thought long about this. Though she could have played the part well, he wasn't sure what Bella knew from Lust, about Ian's life beyond his marriage, and wasn't in the mood to bring her up to speed. He would never be in the mood to talk about it all. Evelyn, for all her faults, knew every detail. And was attractive enough to sell how well he was doing. Or how well he wanted them to think he was doing.

"I went on a date with her the other night. She's quite fun to talk to and prettier than my ex—"

"Is she," Evelyn said, more a statement than a question.

"Quite. She's made a career out of it. Actually I think she'd like to go if—"

"No, it's fine. I'll go."

"Are you sure?" he asked, looking around the room. "You seem busy with—"

"I'm sure," she cut him off, the jealousy clear in her voice. "It's not all about looks. She'll probably say the wrong thing and get you in further trouble…" Evelyn hesitated, her surety morphing to self-doubt. "Wait, when is it?"

Ian's rapidly growing grin vanished. "Friday night. Why?"

"This Friday or next Friday?"

"You're going to sweat through your jacket if you don't calm down."

"I know I say this a lot, but you sound like Pearce."

"And as I have said just as many times, he is quite wise."

They were standing on the front porch of his parents' Craftsman-style house. Ian could hear them within. The music playing, the sounds of conversation, the gentle screams of three- and four-year-olds running about. Ian had refused to knock until he'd gone over everything with Evelyn again.

"My mom's name is—"

"Ruth. Your father Greggory, never Greg. Your brother Dean is married to Susanne and their daughters are Presley and Jada. Can we go inside now?"

"Which daughter is older?" Ian asked.

Envy glared at him through inhuman eyes, before leaning around him and pounding on the peeling door three times.

"There's one thing I neglected to mention. A reminder, really; just a small thing. I'm sure it won't be an issue," she said quickly, not looking at him as Ian bore holes in her head.

"Something other than the entire charity-auction-dance you neglected to mention for the past three months?" Ian asked, still sore she hadn't invited him sooner.

The following Friday, Evelyn and the Spirits would be hosting her first ever auction gala, selling off items she had acquired to raise money for charity. That was what Pride had spent all that time in his room working on, at Evelyn's behest. It's what Gavin was avoiding talking about in the gym, how he'd be helping set up for the event, and what Evelyn was worried about overlapping with this dinner. Once she explained it, Ian understood why he hadn't been invited. He knew the condition he was in when they met him, a depressed substance abuser and a stranger, but it hurt nonetheless.

"Yes," she said to his question.

"What is it?"

"I can't lie to humans."

Ian swore under his breath just as the door opened.

"Ian! I heard that."

"Sorry, Mom," he said, leaning down to hug her.

She was a cheerful woman, almost completely grayed, but that was the only thing about her that showed her age. Though wrinkled, her face was taut and her smile bright. She beamed at him like she hadn't seen him in years. Almost eight months, actually, and it immediately set in. He didn't know quite how much he missed them until the door had opened. His mother looked exactly the same as he had last seen her, and something about that pulled at a familiar warmth in his gut.

Done embracing, she pulled back to observe Envy with a shocked, "*Who* is this?"

The inflection she put on that first word—Ian had spent so much time around Evelyn he had almost forgotten how she looked to everyone else. A woman whose core motive was wanting, and could sculpt her features to her will. She looked every bit of that power and he couldn't help but smile at his mother's approval.

"This is Evelyn. Evelyn, this is—"

"Lovely to meet you, Ruth. I've heard a lot about you," Evelyn said, reaching out a gentle hand and a gentler smile.

Ruth took the hand, only to pull Evelyn around and put her own arm through hers. "And I haven't heard anything about you, but we haven't heard much of anything lately," Ruth said through her eyebrows at Ian. "Pleased to meet you."

She led them into the home while Ian made a face neither one could see, following behind.

The entry gave way to a sitting area and brick fireplace to their right, and the dining room on their left, which led back to the kitchen.

Through the narrow hallway in the middle they caught a glimpse of two children running between doorways when they were met with the onslaught of other guests. A handshake with his dad turned into a hug while his brother made remarks about his haircut.

"It looks more expensive than the rest of your outfit combined."

"It isn't," Envy said, adding to Ian's turmoil. He still hadn't let go that she had paid for everything currently on his person, including his haircut.

"Everyone, this is Evelyn," he said, putting an arm around her. They hadn't discussed this, but Envy cozied into him, both knowing they had to sell this. Ian was thankful for her willingness to participate, showing it with a pinch to her side.

Everyone was cordial enough once they got past her initial looks. His dad looked at his brother, who looked at him. The women were far less conspicuous, asking each other where they had bought their shoes and tops and rings. A meeting ritual among women that Ian didn't quite understand, but he accepted it as a good sign.

In the undertones and the stolen glances, Ian could tell they all had questions. Questions he was determined to avoid this evening.

"How long have you two been together?" Suzanne, his sister-in-law asked.

Envy turned her head to Ian, smiling in a way that said *I can't answer that.*

"Oh, who can really keep track of that anymore," Ian said, trying to be as vague as possible. The frenzy had died down and they all stood there a few moments, waiting on someone to speak.

It was his mother who broke the tension with a smile. "Who could use a drink?"

☦

Evelyn was being stared at by his nieces. Serving wine turned into sitting down for dinner, and Evelyn, next to the head of the table and across from the girls, was enjoying it.

"You're pretty," Jada said.

"Almost too pretty," added Presley.

"*Girls*," their mother chided but Envy was laughing. "I'm sure you're used to it, looking like that," Suzanne said, not with a tint of jealousy but acknowledgment at Evelyn's appearance.

"You know, I find myself in awe of others' beauty more than you'd think," Evelyn said, taking a sip of her wine.

Ian had hardly touched his. After his months of binge drinking, he found it all tasted the same. Mostly, he thought about what he had said to Dr. Bardot in that first session behind her home, and smirked at how right he was.

"What do you do for a living?" Suzanne asked Evelyn.

"I deal in rare antiquities."

"Like desks and tables and such?" his dad asked, interested in the conversation for the first time.

"Mostly, yes," she said.

Ian didn't know that actually, realizing it must have been true or she wouldn't have been able to say it. He kicked himself for not asking more questions about her past, knowing now she couldn't still be living off money from her…past life. Of course she had rolled it into a new career.

"Is that how you two met?" Ruth asked. Everything said was laced with an undertone. His mother knew that wouldn't be the case, though you couldn't tell from the smile that underlined it all.

"No, Mom," Ian interjected, hoping to take the focus off Envy. "I work in private equity now."

"Private equity?" asked Suzanne.

"We buy and sell businesses," said Ian. Keep the answers to a minimum and they'd make it out alright. They didn't need to know he was the lowest person on the totem pole, as long as it sounded good.

"Things seem to be going well, dear." His mother said it with a full smile but other unspoken questions lay beneath it. What he had been doing these past months. Where he had been. If he was okay. He was grateful, at least, that no one was asking the quiet part out loud. They'd assume Evelyn didn't know everything about his life. On the contrary, she knew more than the rest of them combined.

"For more than just us, it seems," Ian said, changing the subject. "Almost forgot to congratulate you, Dean. A master's in Engineering. That's no small feat."

"Just trying to keep the family success story alive," he replied, and immediately realized his mistake. "I mean, err—"

"Dessert, anyone?" his mother chimed in.

After dinner, they moved into the sitting room with a roaring fire while Ruth and Suzanne got the dessert ready. He felt awkward leaving the women to do this while the men went into the parlor but he couldn't split up from Evelyn and he knew they'd kick him out of the cramped quarters if they both went. Moments after taking a seat, almost like it was planned, Ruth came over with a wry smile on her face.

"Evelyn, dear, do you mind lending me a hand in the kitchen?"

No no no, don't go, Ian thought, but couldn't say. "Mom, I don't think she wants to—"

"Nonsense. We've hardly gotten to know her, and I'm sure she'd be more comfortable with us girls than stuck here listening to your dad go on about golf."

Ruth's words carried the weight of a decision already made and Evelyn was half out of her chair before she was done speaking.

"I'll be fine, honey," Envy grinned, brushing a hand on his. "What's the worst that can happen?"

Ian was already thinking of the worst things that could happen and could just make out the beginnings of a question his mom was asking when a blunt pain rattled his knee—

"Hey, man, what the hell?" Dean had swatted him, looking toward the kitchen and back to him.

"What?" Ian asked, shrugging, only to receive a more perplexed expression as his brother leaned in.

"You disappear for eight months, no one can get a hold of you, your house has a foreclosure sign out front, and your wife's living with another man, and *you* show up here, with no warning, an Italian model on your arm and a new wardrobe?" Dean was hissing in a low voice, controlled fury in his eyes.

"That's *what*."

Ian opened his mouth to say something, looking between the two men. His dad was silent but his face said more than Dean could have with words. Ian supposed it would all look extremely odd, but then again, they hadn't been around the past eight months. Not that it was their fault.

"Is she a hooker?"

Ian almost choked. "God, no. She's…" He tried to think quickly but was more distracted by the irony of him having almost brought one. In hindsight, Bella would have been a more believable companion. "She lives in my building. We met a few months back."

"Exactly. *Your building*. Where are you even living? What happened with the house?"

Ian knew he would have to give some answers tonight; he just hoped it wouldn't be like this. "I'm renting on the far side of town. You know things got messy in the divorce. She took the money, I took the house. Just couldn't afford it anymore." He said it clipped, hoping to avoid follow-up.

It was all true at least, just a more simple version. When they split assets, Ian didn't want to give up the house he viewed as his and mortgaged a buyout for her. It was stupid, but he wasn't thinking clearly at the time and it cost him dearly. With his cash depleted and his job gone, everything else went quickly.

"And the hospital visit?" his dad asked, worry and fright in his voice. "We didn't hear from you for months. All we knew was you were carried away in an ambulance. The neighbors said you were—"

"A stress episode. Never thought I'd lose my wife and my house in the same year," he said, another half-truth. He hoped the shame of his words would ward off the questions, but the look of worry on his father's face kept him going.

"Dad, it's fine. *I'm fine.*" He gestured to himself and the kitchen at the same time. "I'm sorry for not calling, I've just been busy trying to get things back on track. Trying to stay focused. I'm sure you can understand that."

Evelyn, please come back. Please.

"Ian, if you need help—" Dean was cut off, but not by Envy returning. Jada and Presley had run into the room yelling "Daddy, Daddy! Play with us!"

One jumped into Dean's unaware lap and the other into their grandfather's. Ian took the opportunity of the chaos to end the conversation as cheerfully as he could imagine.

"Thank you, both. I mean it. But everything's fine now," he said, standing up to rescue Evelyn from his mother.

It turned out she didn't need rescuing. He did.

"...and when he was a baby we'd have to hide the dog biscuits. Just loved eating the things," he heard, walking through the kitchen before clearing his throat.

"Evelyn, a moment?" Ian asked.

She held up a finger for him to wait, leaning in to whisper something to the women, who raised in raucous laughter. Not wanting to be subjected to more, he turned around and went to the dining room, noticing his still full glass of wine on the table. With no desire to drink it, he swirled the red liquid, taking a few deep breaths. The night was almost over, yet he didn't fully want it to be.

It used to feel calming being home. To be in the presence of his loved ones. Yet he hated the circumstances that brought him here. He wanted that calming presence back. That surety of home that nothing can go wrong and everything will be alright. He noticed then, the picture frames on the china cabinet next to the table. Family photos mixed with couple photos of his parents, of Dean and Suzanne. He wondered, as he perused the shelves, what they had done with the photos of him and his ex-wife. Most of the stills were of their family when they were much younger, and then on the far right, he found his favorite. It had always been his favorite.

The two youth-filled faces of his parents, beaming out above two children standing at their shins, all in front of a Christmas tree. Him and his brother. He was ten at the time, Dean seven. He remembered it so well, as the first Christmas in that house, when his parents started making a decent living. Ian didn't know that at the time; he only knew he had more presents under the tree than ever before, and there was a shift in their lives after that. One he couldn't explain other than to say, the house just had more energy to it.

Ian felt Evelyn move into the room as much as he heard her, though she didn't speak, coming to stand at his side, looking at him.

"What?" he asked.

"You're smiling," she said, with one of her own. "Can I ask why?"

He mulled this over for a moment, taking in the room. His mother and sister-in-law could still be seen through the kitchen arch enjoying a glass of wine. His father and brother and nieces were running around the foyer. The fireplace was roaring and there was a faint murmur of conversation over the fainter murmur of music. The house felt full. It felt lived in and loved and it promised of a happy tomorrow. For some of them.

"You told me once that I wanted. That I could hide my want from others but not from you," he said, thinking back to that day in the park. "You were right. This. This is what I wanted. This is what I always pictured her and I having. I wanted a family. I wanted kids, and I wanted to have the house their friends loved hanging out at. I wanted to host our friends on nights like these, and give our kids the same wonderful life I had."

He thought further back, to his childhood. It was not in this home. His parents moved when he and his brother left, downsizing to this more modest suburban one. Growing up, they lived in a neighborhood with kids their age, a wonderland for ten-year-old Ian. Free of the burdens that he didn't know could exist.

"You also told me I had to let that go," he said at last, the smile fading.

"You misinterpret my words." She squeezed his hand to a puzzled and hurt look on his face. "It is good to know what you want. Many never achieve because they have no direction. But wanting something so specific closes you off to the possibility of something equal to, or better than, that."

He shook his head, pursing his lips. It would always come down to this. He didn't want something else: he wanted what he wanted, and he wanted to stop being told he couldn't have it.

"You wanted that future, with her. That is what your heart desires, and has desired for over ten years. I know it is not easy to move past. But you will, one day. Only if you don't give up," she said, with another squeeze.

He felt a pang of guilt there but tried not to let it show. He started to think the guilt would be there for the rest of his life.

"How am I supposed to let go of that? To let go of this?" he asked, looking around once more.

"You allow yourself to believe, with the barest of hope, that something better is possible," she said. "And for the record, you have not lost this. They are right here." Evelyn had grabbed his hand, his other still holding the picture frame. They might be right there, but he didn't know how to close the gap between them.

"Can I ask you another question?" she asked.

"Hmm," he said in heavy contemplation.

"Why are you lying to them?"

"Do you know what it's like having a supportive family?" Ian asked. He supposed she didn't, after all she had been through. It didn't sound like they were given a very loving embrace when brought to Earth.

Envy huffed a laugh. "Are you complaining about them loving you?"

He shook his head. "You don't understand. My brother has a wife and two kids. Student loan debt, no doubt, from that master's program, on top of a mortgage. My parents have only been empty-nesters a few years. Retired. They've waited almost thirty years to be able to live on their terms again, without having to worry about providing for us or raising us. If I told them what's happened…"

"You think you'd be a burden," Evelyn said. Not a question.

"And I would be. They'd never call it that. They'd call it helping me get back on my feet, or say something pitying like *'this is just the season you're in'*." He joked but she wasn't laughing now.

"What if those things are true?"

"Doesn't matter if they are true," he said, putting the picture frame down. "Only matters what my mistakes cost them. And I won't do that to them. They have their own problems, their own lives."

He was staring into the foyer where these very people were playing with his nieces. He wanted to run in with all the joy he once felt spread across his face. He wanted to be the man he was when the girls were born, the uncle who could be carefree and playful and loving without limits.

He knew, just as well, that man didn't exist anymore. Ian looked over to see Envy in her own quiet contemplation, looking at the same thing he was.

"What?" he asked.

"It was my understanding that the purpose of having other humans in one's life was to share the experience in life. Both in burden and in bounty."

Ian exhaled sharply through his nose with a faint smirk. "You speak like Pearce when you get serious," he said.

She just looked up at him with a pleading face that he ignored.

"C'mon, let's go get through the rest of this," he said.

☦

Ian and Evelyn returned to the Victorian home relatively unscathed. He was grateful no one had tried to corner him again after the stint in the foyer, and was able to sneak out when his brother and sister-in-law said goodnight on the pretense of the girls being past their bedtime.

The ride home had been quiet. Ian could tell Evelyn had something on her mind but he was too emotionally exhausted to relieve the tension. Now in the house, they said goodnight, him turning to the narrow corridor leading to his room, and her on the stairs. She stopped short.

"Ian, do you know the worst sin of all?"

"Are you going to tell me right now?" he asked, hoping this could wait until tomorrow.

"It doesn't have an embodiment," she said, skipping past his question. "Not like we do. It is the only desire humans have that doesn't require assistance in corruption. It is the first thing your kind learns in life. When the sun sets, and the moon does not rise, and the howling begins in the brush you cannot see."

A prickling rose on his arms and the back of his neck, the room feeling colder than it had moments ago. She stared at him in wait, a dead expression on her face but a gleam in her eyes when she said: "Fear."

18

"I didn't know fear was a sin," he said. Everyone had heard of the seven deadly sins, even more so of the ten commandments, but he had never heard fear listed in either.

"Is it not? Name what else can corrupt so swiftly. Pride, Lust, Envy, Greed, Wrath, Slovenliness, Gluttony—none of *us* corrupt like Fear."

Ian didn't know what to say to that, the tiredness in his eyes replaced by the hollow of helplessness he had grown so accustomed to. He knew what she was implying; that he was making decisions in fear. But it wasn't her place to tell him how to deal with the parents he had known his entire life. It wasn't her place to put that burden on them. Not wanting to rehash their conversation from earlier, he dismissed it.

"Thank you for tonight, Evelyn," he said.

She dipped her head in a short nod, and turned to go upstairs.

Returned to his room, Ian was preparing for bed when he noticed something amiss. The faint outline of an object on the dresser stood out to him. He hadn't noticed it before leaving that evening, and no one ever came into his room. At least not that he knew of.

Ian moved to the dresser, catching the slight glint of the rectangular object reflecting back at him. In the faint light, he picked up the wooden-framed picture he held just an hour ago in his mother's house. Staring back at him were his youthful parents with him and his brother on a Christmas morning.

19

The morning of Evelyn's auction, Ian awoke to an empty house. He turned his bedroom door handle to the sound of rumpled plastic, a bag hitting the floor. He looked down and picked up what appeared to be dry cleaning, before catching sight of the note.

> *Thought you could use this, just don't outshine me.*
> *-E*

He tore the plastic off the hanger, revealing a sleek black tuxedo, smiling at the ridiculous notion that he could ever outshine Evelyn.

✣

The warehouse in question was unlike what he had pictured. Unlike the bare metal framing and rusted exterior he visited with Bella on their date, Evelyn's 'warehouse' was extravagant. A mural of brick and metal and glass, either built or refurbished sometime in the last decade.

Ian drove Gavin's car to the address he was provided with, Gavin not seeming to care that Ian didn't have a license anymore. The others had ridden together in Pearce's car that morning. Ian turned a corner to a line of cars, their suit- and dress-clad owners heading inside. The Spirits had spared no expense on the evening; even a red carpet greeted him as he exited the black Pontiac and handed the keys to a valet.

Couples filed in around him to the amber-lit interior. He was immediately met with a waiter offering champagne, which he accepted, and began to take in the room around him; the elegance. Evelyn's treasures were positioned throughout in a way to feel natural and used. The room was lit with her chandeliers and embellished with her furniture. Seating corners were created with settees over Persian rugs. Her armoires carried attendees' coats, and an antique banquet table sat at the head of the room.

"Do you like it?"

Ian turned to see Evelyn. She was wearing a black floor-length dress, which hugged one leg and exposed the other before it snaked up her torso and down one arm. His mouth must have fallen open, because she chuckled. "I don't have to wonder if you like the dress."

Ian righted himself, looking away. "Evelyn, it's all—perfect. It's just perfect," he said. "Don't take this the wrong way, but…will the auction even bring in more than this costs?"

She smiled. "Probably not, but I'm not paying for it," she said. "Everything is donated, from the drink in your hand to the table you'll sit at. It's a community event, and luckily, the community has liquor stores and rental companies looking for write-offs," she winked. "And it helps that I own the building, but here," she handed him a paddle with the number 7 on it.

Ian stared at it. "What am I supposed to do with this?"

"You raise it and bid on things."

He was about to remind her he couldn't afford any of this when she excused herself to greet more arrivals. Left without a social crutch, he looked around, verifying he didn't know who any of the guests were. By the looks of them, they must have been the most prominent people in the city, their tuxedos and gowns purchased rather than the rental he was wearing. Wealth dripped off them even in their smiles and their walks.

Just before giving up on a new crutch, Ian spotted Louie and Gavin huddled together in a corner, Louie gesturing with an auction paddle, playing out some unknown circumstance. It was odd to see either of them in formal clothing, Lust's formalwear devoid of stripes or hat, and Gluttony's tuxedo near bursting at the seams through his back, arms, and legs.

Ian wandered over, Louie seeing him before he arrived. "Oh good, you have one. C'mere," he said.

Ian huddled in with them, confused, as Lust continued: "Don't be the first and don't be the last. Look at who's biddin', see how quick they raise their paddles. If it's too quick, hit 'em again," Lust explained.

"Hit who with what?" Ian asked.

"We gotta get these prices up, boyo," Lust said, "make 'em work for it."

"But don't bid on anything that we do," Gavin said. "We want them to think it's just them and someone else who wants it. Too many people will scare them off."

"You're going to artificially inflate the prices?" Ian asked in disbelief.

"*We*," Lust emphasized, rotating his arm in a circle, "are goin' to do our civic duty in raisin' as much money as possible for the causes that be. And by we, I mean *you*."

"I don't have any money!" Ian hissed a little too loudly.

Lust pulled him back down. "Then don't lose. Or win. Don't win, because winnin' is losin.'"

Gavin was nodding along with every word.

"You're not making any sense," Ian said, his face growing hotter.

"I can't explain this any simpler," Lust said and peeked over Ian's shoulder. "Ahh, fack."

Ian shifted to see his boss walk through the door. Greed. "He was invited?" Ian asked.

"Few in the city are better known than Gio," said Gavin. "Even fewer with more money."

19

They watched Greed make his way across the room from them, approaching Pearce, who stood at the bar, smiling. Ian had never seen him do that unless it was with smug denigration. It was wiped away when he caught sight of Gio. The three looked on as Pride tensed, their conversation already one of hostility, Gio leaning in, pleading a case they could not hear. Pearce refused to meet his eye, his lips a tight line and his eyes distant.

Ian's feet were moving before he noticed, heading between the two, unsure of what he was even doing.

"Can I talk to you?" Ian asked Gio.

"We're in the middle of something," Gio said, keeping eye contact on Pearce.

"I know, but it's about the acquisition," Ian said.

That got his attention. As soon as Gio's eyes peeled away, Pearce walked off.

"What is it?" Greed asked.

It was true Ian had questions about the file he'd been working on for the better part of three weeks, though nothing that couldn't wait until Monday. He didn't know why he even wanted to save Pearce, but something told him he should.

"I'm trying to be as emotionless as you suggested, but this one's odd. They have unpaid invoices that are years old, debt that's constantly sold off for pennies, and an entire division with no income, only expenditures. Where is that money going?"

"That is not your concern. Your concern is, *is there room for improvement?*" Gio stated, and Ian faked contemplation, ensuring Pride was far enough away that their conversation couldn't immediately resume. He already knew the answer.

"On the billables, at least. You could outsource the collections to a call center. On the incomeless division, it's impossible to say. It could be R&D, and a necessity to growth."

"Then I suggest your report says that. Now go—"

"Why are you here?" Ian cut him off. God, it felt good to do that for once. "Charity isn't exactly what you're known for."

"Another thing you should learn," Greed said, his smugness returning, "Perception is stronger than truth. Giving back, publicly, is an essential function of capitalism. The people need to know all that money's going to good use. Or at least, that it looks that way."

Without another word, Gio left in search of someone more interesting, right as Evelyn's velvet voice could be heard over the speakers.

"Thank you all for coming to our inaugural gala. I can't thank you enough for your commitment to bettering this city, and this community. Without you, none of this would be possible.

"Our live auction will begin in a moment. As a reminder, tonight's efforts will be dispersed between five charities, all in dire need of funding, so please, don't hesitate to raise those paddles, and if your arm gets tired, you are more than welcome to switch hands."

The crowd gave a haughty laugh before Evelyn thanked them again and the bidding began.

It started slowly. Bottles of wine and comped evenings at fancy restaurants, going for less than one thousand each, but as soon as the small-ticket items ran out, Ian was baffled at the escalation.

A faded blue and white Keshan rug began its bidding at twenty thousand dollars. The personal settee of Gertrude Stein began at thirty thousand, and the chandelier over their heads at fifty thousand. He noticed it as the one that once hung low in Evelyn's own room. Fifty thousand dollars; probably worth more than the house surrounding it, but that wasn't its sale price, just where it started.

Ian could see the bobbing heads of Louie and Gavin roaming the crowd throughout the auction, never staying in one place long. They raised their paddles early and often, getting into bidding wars over antique vases and seventeenth-century traveling chests. They'd stop their bidding at the perfect time, pinning the escalated price on some duped elder.

Unfortunately, it wasn't long before the crowd caught on.

By the time the prized possession of the evening came up, others would not bid if they saw the marked paddles of Lust and Gluttony. They too had noticed this when the American Federalist style banquet table was announced, carved in 1760 and serving as the table in George Washington's very home. Bidding began at one hundred thousand, and no one moved. The air stilled, conversations quieting to muted murmurs. They waited, and waited, and the two spent Spirits eyed Ian like the world rested on his shoulders.

But he couldn't do it. One hundred thousand dollars? He still thought daily about the debt he owed to Evelyn, to the hospital. He couldn't imagine the predicament he'd face if he was on the hook for that much money. He looked back at Louie, the pleading in his eyes at the anticipation of the room. Ian pursed his lips in apology as Evelyn's head swiveled left to right, trying to locate anyone who would bite. Her face was outwardly hopefully but he knew her well enough by now to see the disappointment in her eyes.

She raised the mic back up. "Seventy-five thousand," she said with a cheer, "remember, it's for a good cause."

Still, no one moved. The disappointment gleamed in her eyes and Ian felt a pang of something in his chest, his gut. He couldn't explain why, but he raised his paddle.

"Seventy-five! Do we have eighty?" Evelyn asked, looking around again. It didn't take long before a man in a bolo tie with a hunched back raised his paddle. Evelyn called out again for eighty-five, this time to no takers, a smile growing on his face at the steal of the night.

Evelyn called out a last time, hope in her voice but resignation on her face. The table would sell for presumably more than she paid for it, but significantly less than she had hoped. Just before announcing the sale, Ian saw it out of the corner of his eye. He turned to see the raised arm of Gio, the same playful smile on his lips from all the times he had toyed with Ian. This time, it was directed at the stranger, and it began.

The two went back and forth in the same increments until reaching one hundred and thirty thousand, at which Gio held back, clearly faking disappointment at his inability to stomach the asking price. Evelyn quickly announced an end to the auction, turning to where Gio stood in the audience. He simply raised a glass to her and winked. He knew what they were doing and, for some reason, had joined them in it. Maybe it was a remembrance of past times, or just the further facade of outward charitability, but Evelyn beamed back in thanks.

The evening came to a close as all do, at first a trickle and then all at once. It was 10 p.m. when the last of the guests left. Ian stood around with his housemates as Pearce tallied up what was raised, Louie and Gavin jumping at the bit to hear, rather proud of themselves for their efforts.

"Four hundred and...eighty-two thousand," Pearce said, looking up from his pad with a wide grin.

Evelyn beamed. "Nearly $100,000 for each charity," she said, hand to her mouth.

There was elation in her voice, an air of almost impossibility. Ian couldn't believe it either. Not just at the amount raised in one night, but at who had accomplished it.

"Spectacular," Louie said with a crazed look in his eye.

Gavin was flexing as if he had done it all himself.

"Is this how Gio feels all the time? I'm hard enough to fuck a block of lead. Let's do it again; let's move to semiannual," Lust said.

"You fly around the world for the next six months haggling for items and I'll think about it," Evelyn replied playfully before looking around. "But first, this needs to be cleaned up."

They each took in the war-torn room, littered with cups and flower petals and the occasional spilled drink. The room was completely empty aside from them, and Louie, Gavin, and Pearce had all undone their bowties, shirking their jackets.

Pearce found the janitorial closet first, pulling out an array of brooms, buckets, and mops.

"Where's the wait staff?" Ian asked as Pearce dispersed them.

"Home by now," said Evelyn. "Rentals just like everything else."

She took out her earrings, stowing them in a black clutch, and threw her stilettos to a corner. Gavin must have found the speaker system because a melodic quartet had begun playing overhead, Louie whistling to the tune while folding tablecloths. Ian only now realized who had set this all up, and who would be taking it down. These four were so at ease with each other at times, no expectation or infighting, each pulling their own weight. Ian paled slightly, realizing the only time there was tension it involved him.

"Thanks for coming; it means a lot," Evelyn said. "We'll meet you back at the house."

She began to head away when Ian muttered, "Oh," and she turned back, all eyes in the room tracking back to him. He realized they were waiting for what was wrong.

Ian reached up, scratching the back of his head. "I just…well, I thought I'd stay and help. If that's alright," he said.

No one replied, but Evelyn smiled and nodded, handing him a broom.

20

I did what I could to avoid that night, our plans laid long before our attachments. It is a difficult thing, to willfully hurt another, and its necessity matters not when he would not choose it himself.

It was done.

Ian had spent every moment at work on his project from Gio, unraveling the finances and painting the future that would be their next acquisition. With a few days to spare, he would turn it in. Though the money was an appreciated bonus, that was not his driving force this time. This time, it was the information he was promised.

The folder landed on Gio's desk with a plop, Ian smiling triumphantly in expectation.

"Do you want an award?" Gio drawled.

He did, actually. "We had an agreement," Ian said.

Gio picked up the folder, thumbing through it. "I may be a supernatural creature with abilities you can't comprehend, but osmosis is not one of them. The agreement was for the information to be useful. As I have not read this yet," Gio said, waving the documents. "I can't know if you've held up your end of the deal."

Ian steeled, "You know I have."

20

"No, I do not. You'll get your payment when a decision is made," Gio said, resuming his work in the usual fashion that indicated Ian was dismissed.

Ian didn't move. "When will that be?"

Gio sighed. "I suspect next week sometime, but if you want an advance on it, you can head back to your little love shack. You can have the day off."

Ian stared at him with such confusion, Gio was forced to continue. "I received an invitation for something or other being hosted there tonight."

"What is it?"

"I don't know. I didn't read it."

"Why not?" Ian asked.

"Because I'm not going. *Marcy!*" Gio shouted.

His secretary filed in on swift feet, grabbed him by the arm and ushered him out, ending Ian's work day.

When Ian arrived back at the house, no one could be found. No one except Sloth in his usual place positioned in front of the TV. Ian joined him, taking the open chair. "Where is everyone?"

Sloth grunted in response but even after all these months, Ian couldn't quite translate it the way the others could. A half hour later and midway through a periodical episode, Ian heard the four others emerge from Pride's quarters, Pride himself joining them in the living room.

"Ian, can you assist in moving the television to the attic, and returning the chair to the dining room. We are having guests this evening," he said.

Sloth made another grunting noise that mirrored Ian's own confusion.

"We never have guests," Ian said with furrowed brows. He didn't consider Louie's evening companions "guests" so much as temporary inhabitants who were always gone by the morning.

"We do tonight. Scooter," Pride said, addressing the lazy brute, "you do not have to join if you do not wish, though as always, you will be required in your human form if you choose to attend."

Scooter looked back at the TV as if nothing happened and Pride turned to leave.

"Wait!" Ian called. "Who is it?"

Something about this didn't feel right to Ian. This house was their home, but it was not a place any of them would choose to have visitors. The Spirits had each molded their rooms in their own image in the years they had been there, but the open common areas were as dilapidated as the day Ian moved in. Paint peeling off the walls, cobwebs in the dark untouched corners of the ceiling, and floorboards that creaked at the barest of movements.

"People fundamental to your improvement," Pride said.

Ian screwed up his face at what he felt was an insult. It had been nearly four months in the house and he thought he was doing quite well, all things considered. Before he could ask another question, Louie and Gavin passed the doorway Pearce stood in, heading toward the kitchen and taking Ian's attention with them. One carried a mop and broom, the other a bucket and dustpan. Louie was wearing an apron and rubber yellow gloves halfway up his forearms.

Ian chased after them. "What are you two doing?"

"Chores!" they called in unison.

Hours later, the doorbell rang.

The doorbell never rang. And no one moved to answer.

Ian looked and listened. The home was still. Silent, as if empty. He had been in his room the past few hours, organizing his own modest possessions and getting ready for their guests, unknown if

20

they would enter there or not. Anyone who ever visited the home did so while accompanying another, mostly an evening companion of Louie's, making Ian hesitant to answer the door himself. Solicitors stayed away, presumably due to the rundown exterior and non-existent landscaping.

Wondering who it could possibly be, Ian moved from his room to the front door, stopping to take in a nearly unrecognizable distance in between. The living room had been furnished with chairs and a sofa Ian noted being from Evelyn's room, a centerplace rug underneath. The dining room table was clean, near shining, with polished dark wood under a chandelier he had never before seen lit. The kitchen leading to the foyer had been scrubbed of decades of dirt and grime that once coated its classic, though aged, counters and floors. It would have looked presentable, if everything else were not so austere.

Ian took a peek through the eyehole of the front door, only to find it stained by time and unusable. He could just make out the faint figures of people. Ian unlocked the top latch, turning the handle to welcome their guests.

When he opened the door, he was staring at his parents.

Panic seized him, gaping at the people who should not be there. People who should never have seen where he was living. Their faces quickly moved from excitement to confusion as he stood there not speaking, eyes darting between the two. His instinct pulled the door to him closer, blocking the view of the interior.

"Aren't you going to invite us in?" Ruth asked.

"What're you doing here?" he asked instead, unable to move his feet.

"Well, we were invited of course," his mom cheered. Her eyes darted over Ian's shoulder. "Hello, dear!"

Evelyn had come up from behind him, prying the door from his grip as she smiled back at his parents. "Welcome! So happy you could make it. Please come in."

His parents moved past him, not noticing the look of contempt, of betrayal, on his face, boring into Evelyn. She pointed them to the living room, where Ian could now hear Pride, Lust, and Gluttony out of their hiding.

When they were a few lengths away, he turned. "What the fuck are you doing?" he hissed.

"Keep your voice down. We will talk after dinner," she said.

"*No*, we will talk now—"

"*After dinner*," she shot back and stormed into the kitchen, slowing her gait and relaxing her posture right before turning to rejoin his parents. He slowly stalked after her, cooling his own expression until they could hash it out. He would do what he had to, what he did those weeks ago in his own parents' home, when he feigned that all was right in his world. And he would raise hell after.

☦

His parents were seated on the couch that had spontaneously arrived downstairs in the last few hours. Gavin was handing out finger-food from a silver tray, telling his parents it was gluten-free, as if they would know what that was. Evelyn was sitting across from them pleasantly, while Louie was being himself. He had on a full tuxedo, overdressed to the umpteenth degree, and emanating a rich leather and tobacco cologne Ian had never smelled on him before. He wondered for a moment if this was how the Spirit responded to nerves, only to hear his true intentions.

"You have lovely legs, anyone ever tell ya that?" Lust asked with a smile.

His mother actually blushed, seated right next to his father, who seemed equally enthralled at the Irish accent. His mother looked at her father briefly, touching her hair. "I had my day," she said coyly.

"Oh, I don't think it's over yet," Lust winked at her.

Ian cleared his throat, moving further into the room. The only seat remaining was next to his parents on the couch, with Pride standing at the hearth and Gavin moving to and from the kitchen. He had never seen Gluttony acting this way, though he supposed the Spirit rarely had occasion to.

His parents' eyes had begun roaming the room, up to the ceilings, down the dark passage hallways that veered off, and the floors gapped with age.

"What a…unique place," his dad commented.

"Has a certain charm to it," his mom added. "You all live here?"

Ian tugged at his shirt, readjusting where he sat. "It's temporary. Like I said at dinner, I just need some time to get things back on track."

"Nothing wrong with having roommates," his dad said, looking over at Pride. "After college I lived in a two-bedroom condo with eight guys. We alternated sleeping in the tub."

"You were twenty-three," Ian said, tired of their incessant optimism.

"And you work for a private equity fund. I'm sure you'll be making millions in no time," his dad smiled.

Pride moved to sit beside them. "Oh, Ian's just an analyst right now, but it gives him plenty of time with his therapist."

Pride smiled as Ian's stomach hollowed out. So that's what this was—forcing him to confront his life. Evelyn had gone completely still at his side, their legs touching but a trench between them. His mother, on the other hand, was beaming.

"Oh, honey, that's fantastic. Your father and I have been going for years, and I know you were hesitant about marriage counseling with Laura but—"

"Thank you," he cut her off, not wanting to hear another word. Not wanting another word said that could be used against him.

Ruth took the hint, returning to musings of the house and complimenting Gavin on his cooking. They didn't directly speak again until the three peeled off for a tour of Ian's room, an awkward stiffness between them.

It was broken by his father when they entered his sparse room, "Nothing to be ashamed of, son. I'd have killed to live in a house like this with a bunch of friends at your age."

"They're not my friends," Ian said, deciding not to elaborate, "and I'll be moving in a few months. Can we not talk about this?" His temper was growing again, willing him to ruin the night.

His father turned his palms out. "Okay, it's just…" he trailed off.

Ian took a deep breath. "What is it?"

"They seem like nice people, son, like they truly care about you."

Ian left that hanging between them. He didn't know how to tell him that they weren't people at all, and they weren't helping by choice, either. They had moments, certainly, where Ian forgot who and what they were, where he forgot that the arrangement was an obligation more than anything else. But at the end of the day, their true colors would always shine.

His mom neglected to mention the photo that rested on his dresser, so clearly stolen from her house, seemingly more happy about it than upset, and the tour and the night ended before he knew it. He hoped it could be a better goodbye and knew he wouldn't be able to deliver it, his anger at the others sitting just below the surface and inching closer. Most farewells were said in the living room before Ian and Evelyn guided his parents to the foyer.

Ian kept it together until the moment the door closed, waiting just long enough to hear his parents' car doors close.

"What the hell was that?" he asked Evelyn in disbelief.

She kept her gaze steady and her voice firm as she recited words that did not sound her own: "What needed to happen."

"Do not yell at her," Pride's voice boomed from the doorway, "She did as she was told."

Ian turned, his disappointment growing to fury. "Told by who? You?"

he demanded.

"Yes," Pride said with finality.

Evelyn excused herself, muttering something about assisting Lust with the cleanup, her head low as she left them.

"And what gives you the right to invite them here without my permission?" Ian seethed at Pride.

"We do not need your permission to do what we believe is in your best interest," he said.

"Humiliating me in front of my family is *not* in my best interest!"

Pride's face hardened, his relaxed posture sharpening. "Stop acting like you're too good for this."

"This is the advice from *Pride*?" he yelled back.

"This is the advice to a man who has too much of it!"

"I've been in this house months—*months*! Evelyn, Louie, Gio—I could tell you exactly how they've helped me. What have you done other than give orders and half-assed truths?" Ian was seething, shouting what he had felt for a while now.

Evelyn had helped him with his desire, his nightmares, even his confidence. Louie had gone from a slimy eel of a devil to a confidant in the one area he had never been able to talk about or share with anyone. Louie had transformed his life in probably the biggest way of anyone. Gio, though reluctant and for his own self-interest, had given him a job and his time. Significantly more than Pride.

"You are blind to your own sins, Ian. The embodiment of your trespasses stands before you, lives under the same roof, and still you do not recognize it."

"What are you talking about?"

"Your life! It did not fall apart because of the decisions of your wife, or because of your job. Your friends. Your family. Your life has become what it is because of pride," the demon sneered, showing more emotion than he had in the past five months. "Your pride kept you from asking for help. How many times did you turn down marriage counseling? How many times could you have asked for help at work? How many times could you have called your family? Four months, Ian, and they only now know where you live."

"You have no idea what you're saying. You weren't there," Ian said, ignoring too many of the statements.

"No? So you are not the man who is too good to live in this house? Too good to be a subordinate? Too good to ask out women you deem below you? What is good enough for you? What does a man, who has nothing, deserve?"

Ian turned to leave. "I don't have to listen to this," he said, and Pride turned into smoke. A disillusioned matter, morphing rapidly, moving quicker than any human could, he reappeared before Ian, blocking his exit.

"You cannot run from me like you do from yourself," Pride said, inches from his face. "You feared having to be a man who needed help, and you became a man who couldn't live unless he received it."

Ian swung, swiping through smoke as Pride morphed again.

"Coward!" Ian shouted.

Pride did not reappear but his voice echoed through the room, the deep haunting voice of his true form: "*Coward*, says the man who can't face his own mistakes."

"At least I didn't lock mine in the basement."

Suddenly, Pride reappeared, half turned to him. "Now who's the one who doesn't know what they're talking about?" He seethed it, half accusatory and half in question. There was fear in his eyes. Fear that Ian knew the truth.

He didn't, but he could piece together enough. He knew Wrath was down there and he knew Gluttony didn't blame her for it. He knew whatever the reasoning, it had resulted in the last person in Ian's position ending up significantly worse off than they had started. And

20

he knew Pride lay at the center of it all. He took a shot.

"You can keep her down there as long as you'd like, it won't bring him back," Ian said.

There was a look of murderous contempt on Pride's face, so glowering Ian would have thought him the incarnation of Wrath itself if he didn't know better. And something else, flickering just before Pride vanished again. Something that almost looked like regret.

Ian spun around, looking from floor to ceiling and back again, but he could feel the absence in the air. An absence that would not be filled.

21

Spring was in full bloom when Ian arrived at his latest appointment with Dr. Bardot. The planters outside her back office, once wilted and dying, now showcased an array of white and yellow and pink. Their meetings together had grown to a welcomed comfort, one he actively desired after the other night.

Unable to talk to anyone about what had happened, about the betrayal he felt, he had had little exposure to the Spirits or anyone else since their fight. Pride sequestered himself back to his quarters, and Evelyn was off on some new trip Ian suspected hadn't been planned until that night. Lust and Gluttony, though not as directly involved, had actively hid the evening's intentions from him and Ian had no desire to talk to either.

"I think I chose wrong," Ian said to Bardot, now settled in her office.

"I'm not sure I follow," Bardot replied.

Ian was looking out the window, at the colors arranged in the sun, as he thought of their last meeting.

"You pointed out the crossroads I was at, at trusting those around me," he said. "I started to, and for some time it seemed to go well, until it didn't."

"And now you regret it?"

"What else am I to feel, if every time I trust it leads to this?" he asked.

Bardot took a moment, processing something he could see in her eyes. It was brief, and whatever it was, she didn't follow it.

"How's your mental health?" she pivoted.

"My mental health?"

"Don't act so surprised. It's why we started these conversations, if you recall."

When he had attempted to take his life. That was why they were still meeting, though it rarely felt that way. She cut to the chase now, "Do you still have thoughts of suicide?"

He returned his gaze out the window, unsure how to be truthful. For the most part, he'd had good days. He didn't think about taking his life any more. However, he thought of something else. He would sit and think of what it would take to start again, fearful of that day. The last time he attempted suicide, it was at the tail end of losing his support system. Still unwilling to display his mistakes to his family; unable to discuss them with anyone else, and he knew his current situation was even more fragile. A group of demons each with their own agenda, a job he didn't earn, a therapist on someone's payroll, and a family as much on the outskirts as ever.

Bardot took his silence as an answer. "Ian, it's not a sign of weakness to acknowledge if you do. It's a good marker for knowing when to reach out for help before you truly need it."

Bardot cared, he knew she did. He could hear it in her voice and see it in her actions. But that glint behind her eyes returned, worry behind her words.

"I thought we agreed to be straightforward with one another," Ian said, dodging her statements. "Why are you asking me about this?"

The look just beyond her eyes finally broke through and Ian saw her give in against her better judgment. "These thoughts of distrust lead to a topic I'd planned to go over today," she said.

Ian held her stare, a question in his eyes, at the slight shake in her voice that put him on edge.

"I refrained from this sooner because I feared it would trigger a detrimental response. I wanted to be sure you were in a more...stable condition, but given the state of things, I think it's time we discussed your ex-wife, Laura."

The state of things?

"What about her?" he asked.

"Correct me if I'm wrong, but I don't think the attempt on your life was about your firing, or the foreclosure, or anything else. I think it was about her. Betrayal is a common feeling in divorce, one that's rising here again, and one that's not always accurate."

Ian's eyebrows narrowed. "What would you call being cheated on and lied to?"

"A breach of trust, undoubtedly. A moral failure. But in certain circumstances, I'd call it one person's side of a story," Bardot said, stone-faced.

She gave him the room to take in that statement, to capture the reality of it, and release the anger it brought.

"So this is my fault?" Ian asked.

"It is likely the result of both of your actions, but Laura is not my patient," said Bardot. "It would be remiss of me if our time together concluded without you facing your portion of the divorce. No matter what our partners do, we make choices ourselves."

Ian was trying, more than he ever had before, to see it their way. He thought of his fight with Pride, who had echoed these same sentiments just a few nights before, and the hard truths that lay there. How Ian had refused to ask for help when he needed it most, how he had turned down marriage counseling, though it didn't seem like that to him at the time.

"How am I supposed to face my faults, when all I see are hers? I made mistakes, I know that, but not more than her," he said.

"That is a contest that no one can win. Pointing to her faults will make you feel vindicated, but it will not heal your emotional wounds, Ian."

"What will?" he asked earnestly.

Ian knew he could not fix the past; he also knew he didn't want the same future. He'd asked Evelyn this same question once, tears brought to his eyes when she had answered with the one thing he wasn't willing to give.

"I think, to acknowledge what you would have done differently would be the acknowledgment of what you could improve. To give you the confidence that if put in that position again, you'd choose a different path," she said. "And if you're willing to tell me about those choices, I'd like to help."

Ian thought about this proposal, one truth standing out above the rest: He was tired. He was tired of always fighting to prove he was right; that if everyone had the same consensus, perhaps, he needed to listen.

And so, he told her. He told Dr. Bardot of how he met Laura that first year of college. Young love, swept in a frenzy of equalized dreams. How they had been each other's firsts, and talked of being each other's lasts. How so much of their lives overlapped in belief, they laughed at where they differed. How the early years of their marriage were what others longed for. He told her of how they started the company, a bootstrapped venture out of their one-bedroom rental, Ian the advisor, his wife setting up appointments. How they celebrated being able to hire a true receptionist, for Laura to chase her own ambition. He told Bardot of the long hours he worked, and the intentions behind it. Of the life he wanted to buy for the both of them, and the rift that unshared vision brought. Hesitantly, he spoke of the desires she needed filled, and the inability he felt in doing so. How she scaled back her adventurous asks, down to therapy, down to a conversation, until she stopped asking all together. He told her how he had tried, at the end, to turn things around. To be the husband he once was, realizing only now why it was too late. How he had already lost her. When he was done, he didn't need Bardot, or Pearce, or anyone else to tell him where it had gone wrong, long before she left.

He was surprised how good it felt to talk about it; more than good. For over a year, he had hidden so many aspects of his past from anyone who inquired. Shelled up in his truths, unable to face what might have been false. So much of it he had never told his wife, wishing, falsely hoping, she'd know his intentions without him voicing them. What he would give to go back and change that. Someone knew though, now, and he'd take that.

Bardot didn't write a single note while he spoke, listening intently at every hard-earned word Ian let go.

When he finished his tale and the silence stretched between them, he uttered the two words that had been said to him so often. "Your turn."

She smiled. "Do you need me to tell you what you already know?"

"It couldn't hurt," he said. He wanted to hear her thoughts, even if they were uncomfortable.

Bardot nodded. "We all want things. Just because we do not receive them, it does not indicate life cheated us. We can control our attitude and our effort, but people, much like outcomes, cannot be controlled."

If only he'd acknowledged that years ago. "Any other thoughts?" he asked.

"Yes," she said. "I think that was our best session yet, and I'm very proud of you." The therapist had melted away, just for a moment, and he saw the person before him. Someone who looked at him with empathy and compassion. Someone who wanted the best for him without other pretense. It made him uncomfortable.

Ian looked at the clock, approaching the time she normally produced the medical container to have him tested. He prodded her toward it, having done enough growth for one session.

"No cup this week?" he asked.

Bardot pursed her lips. "Ian, I am very proud of the progress you have made, and wish we could continue, but we discussed what we did today due to this being our last session."

Ian straightened in his chair. That couldn't be right. June. He always had until June—the six-month cutoff. This was too early. He shook his head reflexively. "We have two more months?"

The look on her face never changed. Lips still pursed, ready for bad news. "I'm afraid the program is being shut down."

"But why? You're doing good here. You're helping people. You're helping me," he pleaded. The first time in months he had been able to open up, bare what he had hidden for so long, and now it was all going away.

"It's not my choice," she said. "The hospital's parent company was purchased by a firm, and they're reducing budgets, not just at our hospital but across all of our sister programs as well..."

She continued on, but Ian didn't hear her. The last sentence bolted shock through his mind. Only her silence when she stopped speaking brought him back into the room. He looked up.

"Who bought it?" he asked.

"A local private equity firm."

Although he knew the answer, he asked it regardless. "What is the name?"

☦

Ian moved as fast as he could, hoping, wishing it wasn't true. That it could be stopped. That it could be undone. He stormed to the downtown building, rushing past those waiting for the elevator, and headed for the stairs, climbing three at a time all the way to the penthouse.

To Greed's floor.

The staircase door flung open with a bang, startling the usually aloof receptionist. Ian didn't look at her as he headed for Gio's office, her pleas and demands to stop falling deaf on his ears. Another rush of doors.

There he was, sitting behind his desk, a look, smug with contempt, radiating through his eyes.

"What did you do?" Ian moved across the room, was right in his face, holding him by the tie, though he knew what Gio had done. The deception he had planted. From the first day Ian went to work, he had this planned, had handed him the files and let Ian unravel the rest. Ian knew better and did it anyway.

"What did *you* do?" Greed replied with a cruel smile, his voice an undisturbed velvet.

"You bought the hospital? But why? What need do you have for it?" he demanded, pushing the man against the bookcase.

"Profit, of course. You did such a thorough job of outlining how we could cut budgets, who was expendable. I just followed your instructions."

"I didn't know it was for this!" Ian shouted, rage mixing with confusion.

Greed leaned in further, mere inches from his face. "And I always told you to ask better questions."

Ian reeled, his grip loosening.

Gio took the moment to gently pry Ian's fingers from his collar before reaching down and pressing the conference button.

He had done this. He had been warned so many times, and had not listened to any of them.

"See, this is just like your kind. No remorse when you think it can't affect you. No remorse when you thought it was other people's jobs on the line. Their incomes. Their *houses*. How quickly that changes

21

when it's your life."

Ian went slack. *That would mean...*

"Oh, didn't you know? That pit you call a house is property of the hospital. An asset I now own," Greed said, and looked at his watch. "The others should know by now. I suspect they'll be packing as we speak."

"What are you going to do with a rundown mansion? You hate it there."

He didn't understand, he couldn't understand. *Why. Why do this?*

Greed shrugged. "Demolish it. Build some condos. Apartments, maybe. Multifamily is all the rage right now."

"You're a cruel bastard. They should have condemned you to hell."

"And you're a deadbeat who's failed at everything in life. Couldn't even kill yourself properly," Greed said as security rushed through the doors, grabbing Ian by the arms. "Look on the bright side—you are good at something. Unfortunately for you, it cost you your home."

22

We've spent nearly three centuries together. In our time, we ourselves felt what we believed to be the full gauntlet of human emotions. Love and loss, grief and hope. Surprise, triumph, and anger. Fear was not one of them; not until now. Curious it was, to see it interact with Pearce. How he cast himself to the humans, cast every inch of his forbearance aside in his threats and in his promises, should he not find what he sought.

Ian didn't mean to do it. It wasn't a conscious choice he made when he left Gio's office. Numb in thought and feeling, one action leading to the next, guided by panic of when it would hit, of when he had to face what had happened—and he sought not to.

Cars and people passed him in a blur on the streets. He was in the same place he'd been four months prior, only worse. Jobless, friendless, and now the one who had done the betraying. Tears welled in his eyes as he thought what it would be to face them. To face Pearce. The Spirit's words rang in his ears: *you do not know what he is capable of,* Pearce had said. The embodiment of Pride, who called Ian out for the very things that led to this. How many warnings had he refused to heed, had he turned into opportunities to fight, rather than listen?

Evelyn's own warnings followed in his mind, the pleas to trust her,

22

to trust them. At her behest, Ian had bettered his relationship with Louie, asked Pearce for help, opened up about his marriage, but he had never trusted them, not really. Doing the bare minimum needed to keep up appearances while he focused on what he thought would truly gain him freedom—his work with Greed. Blinded by his anger at Pride and not seeing what was right in front of him. Now, he had further stripped that freedom from them, taking their home in the process.

He would not call his parents, his brother, tell them he had lost what little he still had left. They were so proud, of his growth, of his job, of the girlfriend they thought he had. It was all a lie. How could he tell them he had squandered the last bit of grace that had been lent to him?

He couldn't. He wouldn't.

As if on cue, his phone rang. Ian looked down at an unsaved number, knowing who it would be. Dread flooded him as fast as the blood left his face. He sent it to voicemail, unable to take the words that Pearce would have for him. Not moments after ringing ended, it sounded in his head. The unmistakable reverberation of the Spirit.

"We know what happened. Where are you?"

Ian tried to expel the thought, to expel Pearce from his mind. He thought to the night in the club. The night Gavin told him how he invited them in, opened his mind with his self-pity, his self-consciousness, but Pierce broke through it all. He rattled off lie after lie, saying it would be alright, that Gio had deceived them all. That they didn't blame Ian. *How could they not?*

He squeezed his eyes shut and focused on anything other than himself, on tuning out the voice. He channeled all the anger and hatred he had toward the Spirit, toward Gio, toward the lies and deceptions, the months of poking and prodding at his life and he raised a wall between him and it.

The last thing he heard before the connections closed was Pride saying, "Do not do this."

Ordering him around—that's all he ever did.

Ian had his own money, which he used to get the room. To buy the bottles and the pills. To escape. Door locked behind him, he sat on the edge of the bed, as he had four months prior, and stared at the now empty bottle of pills. It couldn't go down fast enough, as he chased the pain with the burning sensation of relief, yet it didn't take long. He knew from the last time, it never took long. He felt himself slip from the bed as he thought how much easier this would be. *For them.* For his family to not have to worry about him anymore. He didn't think about Laura last time, but he did now. Relief swept over him, realizing she'd never have to see him like this. How he'd never have to explain himself.

There was a pounding on the door. Someone shouting. He couldn't make out the words. Not his problem. None of it would be his problem if he could just fall asleep. He felt the pull heavy on his body, dragging him into the floor. In moments he would seep into it and he would be greeted by silence. By peace.

It wasn't that he wanted to die. It was simply that he wanted to shut it off. He wished they would allow him, whoever it was that broke into his room.

Let them take his belongings, let them have his body. They seemed to want it and he didn't care, not as they grabbed him, frantically tore at him. By the arms first, then the neck—the head. The face. The only fight he put up was ever so slight, when they brushed his eyelids up, chasing away his peace. Light streamed in, blinding him to the blurry silhouette outlined through the open door. Ian could not see a face. He did not need to. Recognition hit him as the familiar ghost called out, shouting through the dense space between them, eternity away, though he lay in their arms.

His body lifted and he heard weeping, and did not know if it was him or the man, before the dark claimed him.

22

Ian awoke to the familiar white and gray paneled ceiling he had hoped never to see again. He blinked slowly at first, then rapidly, trying to expel the blur lingering in the room. To his right, he heard the shifting before he saw them, and turned his head to see Pearce, Louie, and Evelyn in his hospital room.

"Mornin', boyo," said Louie, though it lacked its usual spark. He was the only one who spoke, and the only one pretending to smile, though his other features sagged. Pearce had the fitful look of regret Ian had only seen once before on his face, and he could tell Evelyn had been crying. Though she covered it well, she couldn't hide the redness of her eyes and the slight dip of her mouth.

Ian breathed in sharply, overwhelmed at the new scenery, at the unspoken words, at the weight of his new reality. At what he had tried in the fog of the prior days, rushing back to him.

"What're you doing here?" Ian croaked. His mouth was drier than expected.

Pearce moved to his bed table, grabbing the glass of water waiting for him. They did not answer him as he drank in shallow gulps.

Setting it down, he asked what he truly wanted to know. "How did you find me?"

"You forget whose name is on your bank account," Pride said, shifting his gaze to Louie and Evelyn. "Can you two give us a minute?" A statement more than a question.

They nodded and moved to the door.

"Can we get you anything?" Louie asked, looking his way.

It was difficult to hold that gaze, seeing the hurt that lay beneath. More pained than the night Ian had accused him of so much, more shame that he had caused it. Bella had been right, and Ian hated how long it took him to realize it. Ian just shook his head, his eyes instinctually moving to Evelyn, who tried to feign a smile before leaving.

"You gave us all a rather large scare," Pride said.

Ian didn't have the energy to be angry at those words. The words that implied the same thing he thought since the first day he met Pride; that his life was only worth as much as their freedom. He no longer felt that way toward the others. Pride, though, was a different story.

Ian sat, exhausted, not saying anything.

"What were you thinking?" Pride asked.

Ian mustered all the energy he could. "You don't get to make this about you."

"Is it so selfish to want you not to die?"

"If you cared whether I lived or not, you should have shown it sooner," Ian said, thinking back to their fight. To the words he shouted in a rage. To the feeling he still had. Pride had never shown the attention to him that Lust had, nor even a fraction of what Evelyn brought forth.

Pride exhaled sharply, closing his eyes. Ian could see the exterior begin to fracture.

"I was hard on you because I saw so much of myself in you. And when Gio got involved…" Pride trailed off.

"Enough of this. What happened between you two?" Ian asked.

Pride took a deep breath. It hurt him, to face this, to admit whatever this burden was that he carried.

"I just destroyed a charity that turned my life around, and possibly collapsed the local healthcare system," Ian said as Pride side-eyed him. "I'm sure whatever it was isn't that bad."

Pride thought for a moment, chewing on something invisible, stress rippling across his jaw and sadness filling his too dark eyes.

"We were—still are—oil and water," he finally said. "We have so much in common, but nature rejects our union. Every Spirit of Greed I have been paired with, it has ended disastrously. This last one, though maybe not even the worst one, was the final straw. The first day you arrived, you asked why we didn't treat you the same as the last person to inhabit the house."

Ian remembered well. It was possibly the only compliment Pride had ever paid him, and hardly one at that, implying he was in a better position than the fifty-five-year-old who had spent more than thirty years in prison. Ian nodded.

"He died," Pride said, letting the statement linger in the air.

"Did you—" Ian began to ask.

"Might as well have. We set him up."

Pride's voice faltered, and for the first time since meeting him, he lowered his gaze to the floor. Ian's heart sank with Pride's face, the torment and guilt flush on his features.

"His name was Thomas. He came to us after serving his time in prison for manslaughter, having accidentally killed someone in a police chase. Thomas had robbed a small municipal bank and was fleeing when he ran a red light, hitting a woman in her car. She died instantly." Pride took a moment, before continuing. "He was doing well, I thought. We were nearly at the end of our time with him, and I...I made a mistake.

"In my nature, and in Gio's, we placed a wager on Thomas's ability to be corrupted by Wrath. I was certain this was not possible. Thomas hated what he had done. The guilt of what had happened when he was a young man. He would never take another life. He was not violent, but I overlooked one detail."

Pride was yet to meet his gaze, clenching and unclenching his fists, moving his hands to his pockets and out again, empty.

Ian didn't speak. He knew his question would be answered. He knew Pride was taking the time he needed to admit this fault.

"I overlooked his ability to hate himself," Pride said, and Ian understood.

He understood what it meant to hate one's self. To hate the decisions he was making even when he knew he should be making different ones.

To hate that he stayed in bed when all he wanted to do, with every ounce of will he possessed, was to get up. He understood the hate that crippled his ability to better his life, not knowing where to start.

"When Thomas took his life, I knew what we did was wrong. I knew I made the wrong choice, and I vowed to change. To be to humans what humans are to each other," Pearce said. "Gio disagreed. He believed then, as he does now, that humans are corrupt by default. That it is not for any reason but their own doing that they stumble." Pride turned to Ian now, a faint glimmer in his eye.

"Although all beings have choices, I find you humans lean in the direction you are pushed. If you are given the ability to do what is right, you will do that. If you are given the ability to do what is wrong, you will weigh it against what you would gain, and act accordingly. That decision is made ever easier if what you can gain far outweighs what you can lose. Thomas gained peace, in a situation he should have never been presented with. He lost his life, and our sentences were extended. Not that Gio cares," he huffed a laugh, tears faint in his eyes.

"And Wrath was locked away," Ian said, but not understanding. "But why wouldn't Wrath just be sent back to—wherever you are from?" Ian asked.

He noticed Pearce had relaxed slightly, a faint slack in his shoulders, an open book Ian had never seen.

"I thought she would be," Pride said. "I thought we all would be. It was argued that if we were sent back, we would not have learned, and thus, the original point of sentencing would be null. This is not merely a prison—it is our rehabilitation. To learn the plights of humans. And I fear we may never accomplish it."

Ian looked at Pride, waiting until their gazes met. "I think you're closer than you know," he said.

Pride gave a weak smile, trying to keep his composure.

"All these months. Did you avoid me because you thought you'd be

22

the reason I tried to take my life again?" Ian asked.

This time, Pride did not move to answer his question. A slight fear welled in Ian that the stone face would return, the polished facade of indifference that held him at arm's length all this time.

When Pride spoke, he asked a new question. "In all our years, do you know how many lives we have saved?"

Ian knew they had been here for quite some time. Centuries, in most cases. His mind still in a fog, he couldn't trace the thought much further. "Hundreds? Thousands?"

Pride huffed another small laugh, one of incredulity. "We never have," he said, in a voice so soft Ian almost didn't catch it.

It was quiet a moment more before he continued, "They were not all like Thomas. Some went back to prison. Some gave in to their addictions, their abusive partners. Their old friends and poor habits. In the end, not a single life has ever been deemed remediated."

"Deemed by who?" Ian asked.

There was a knock on the door and Pride straightened up, the tension and poise returning to his posture as the moment was lost.

Louie and Evelyn entered the room with steaming cups of tea, placing one by his bedside.

"Have you asked him yet?" Evelyn said to Pearce.

"Not yet."

"After all this time I'd have hoped you'd stop talking as if I'm not right here," Ian said in a lethargic tone. Exhaustion was beginning to wear on him, beckoning him back to sleep.

"Sorry, love: Pearce wanted to be the one to ask," Evelyn said with a sheepish grin, "Didn't want to give it away."

Ian turned back to Pearce, fighting his eyelids. "Ask me what?"

The man's normally stone face had shown a litany of emotions today Ian had never seen from the Spirit before, another one crossing his face now. Hesitation.

"We—we aspired for you to join us at the house for a meal. It would be a shame if the last memory there was one of—compunction."

"When?" Ian asked. He would go; he wanted to. He wanted to be there now, in his bed, not in this cold apathetic room. He wanted to hear Evelyn's footsteps pace across the attic, Gavin's muffled symphony, Louie's shameless encounters. He wanted to wake up and watch TV on a small colorless device, sitting in the silence of Scooter. He wanted to tell them of the safety they offered, of how wrong Pride had been only moments before.

"When you're better," Pearce said, moving to stand up.

Ian's eyes were closed now, drifting fast as he thought of being in the house. He vaguely felt the faint press of lips against his forehead, Evelyn muttering her well wishes, followed by the sound of withdrawing footsteps. He wanted them to wait, to tell them one last thing, to thank them for fixing the mistake he'd tried to make twice now, but they were already gone by the time he managed a whisper, just under his breath.

"You saved my life."

23

When Ian arrived at Naferty Lane, he found he'd never been so nervous to enter a place he'd felt so at ease in the past. It had been one week since that morning in the hospital. Ian and Evelyn worked out the details and now he stood on the front porch of the house he once lived in, wondering if he should knock or walk right in. He had lost his key somewhere between the dingy motel and the hospital, and the clothes on his back were as rigid as the night he went to the club with Pearce and Louie.

So nervous, he didn't notice the familiar black town car parked out front. An itch formed above his ear and he reached up to scratch it when the front door opened, Evelyn standing there in her usual attire that faded anything behind her. A grin met him, and he returned it, though more sheepish than he would have liked.

"Thank you for coming," she said, to which he didn't know how to respond. It didn't feel like he was doing them a favor. He had craved the familiarity of the space since the moment Dr. Bardot gave him the news one week prior.

"Where is everyone?" he asked.

"Waiting for you," she said simply, as if their whole world revolved around him.

They made their way to the dining room that had never been used in the four months they had shared the living space. He turned the corner into the open high-ceilinged room, to see the five Spirits seated. And the once caregiver of the home, Claudia, sitting at the head of it. Catty corner to her was Sloth, in his Spirit form.

"Hello, Ian," Claudia said.

He stopped in his tracks. "I—I didn't expect you," Ian replied, looking between them all.

"We were expecting you, though. Take a seat, please," Claudia said, gesturing to the last remaining chair.

The room felt cold with stillness. Pride sat to her right, his positioning and silence shouting that, for once, he was not the leader of the room. Claudia was, and Ian feared what that meant.

"Do you know why I'm here?" she asked.

"I have a suspicion," Ian said. Dread flooded him, waiting for the shoe to drop. For her to rip the last piece of hope from him. She simply smiled.

"And what is that?" she asked, a coy spring to her question.

"You are their…you oversee their sentencing," Ian said, wanting for everything to break eye contact from her, to be comforted by the soft gaze of Evelyn or the humorous smile of Louie. He could feel their eyes on him, but could not look their way. He feared giving this woman any ammunition, any sign that he cared for what happened to them.

"That is correct. I am the Spirit of Charity, and these," she said, gesturing around the table at the others, "are my wards. Or, they were."

Ian broke the piercing eye contact to glance around the room. The others were all still, but their faces, each of them, shy of Scooter, had a faint smile.

"I don't understand," Ian said.

"You know, we are always watching, Ian. We may not always be seen, we may not always be heard, but try to take some comfort in this—*you always were*," said Claudia. "You made a confession in the hospital. One ever so slight. Do you remember it?"

Ian knew what she was referring to. Even in the haze of the drugs and the exhaustion, he remembered. This, he could never forget. Ian nodded to her.

"Did you mean it?" she asked. There was true curiosity in her voice, but also a weight to it. As if the answer were not just an answer, but a determination. Unable to find his voice, he nodded again.

"What does this have to do with anything?" Ian asked, still unsure what burdens could be had if he answered incorrectly.

Claudia's face was stern, a magistrate waiting to pass judgment. "It determines what happens next," she said, and asked again, "Did you mean it?"

This time he answered without hesitation, "Yes. They saved my life, more than once."

A faint smile broke Claudia's face and something in the room shifted. Ian couldn't see it, or hear it, he only felt it, and when he turned to Pearce, the Spirit of Pride had a tear running down his cheek.

"I don't understand," Ian repeated.

"Don't you?" she asked, her chin pointing a different direction than the eyes she had on him.

Ian looked back at Pearce, it clicking as they locked eyes. "You're free," he breathed.

"We are," Pearce said. "Thanks to you."

An involuntary laugh came from Ian. "I didn't do anything."

"You tried," Pearce said, "You'd be surprised how few are capable of that."

Ian felt the prickle behind his eyes, stopping himself at the flurry of questions he still had. How little made sense to him.

"The hospital. You said you had never saved anyone before. If I am the first…" Ian trailed off.

"The quota was one. It was only ever one," Pride said, resignation in his voice. Pain lay there, but joy as well.

"Well, my work here is done," Claudia said, standing and hesitating for only a moment as they all joined her. Before she could continue, Ian cut her off.

"Wait. Greed—Gio," Ian said. "What of him?"

The matron pursed her lips. "It is our understanding that the Spirit of Greed was exactly that in his lackadaisical effort. We have different plans for him that need not worry you—but rest assured, he has been dealt with," she finished as if that was that, and turned to Pride.

"Pearce, I can't say it has been a pleasure, but it has certainly been an experience. If we meet again, I trust it will be on positive terms," she said through her eyebrows, though a faint smirk rested on her lips.

"You were a far more generous host than we could have hoped. Thank you," Pearce said.

Claudia inclined her head, saying to Ian, "I hope these improvements are permanent, though always remember to seek help before it is required."

With a head tilt from the others, including a stunned Ian, she was on her way.

They stood in silence, casting awkward glances around until Pearce motioned the group to sit. Ian's nerves were on end again as they resumed their positions around the ornate table. The five of them surrounded him. This time, he was placed at one head of the table, Pride at the other. Evelyn, Louie, Gavin filled in the spots between, but Scooter made sure to grab the one to Ian's left. Months ago the gentle giant could hardly be in a room with him; now he never wanted to leave his side. In spite of all that had happened, they were having a meal together, almost like a family.

Pride cleared his throat, his features steeled once again after their conversation outside. "Much has happened this past month that you are not up to speed with," he said and Ian's body grew colder. Nothing reeled through his head, no expectations, yet it was history that told him what came next would be bad. Would be another dent in his hopes that never came to fruition.

"You're leaving," was all Ian could bear to say. He knew this day would come. That he would lose them. He just didn't care all those months ago.

"We are," Pride confirmed, "To our new house."

Ian shot up straight, confused. A smirk was growing on Pride's face, but Ian couldn't figure out why. Ian looked to Louie, then Evelyn, who both bore the same pleased expressions.

"But your sentences were commuted. I thought you were free to go back?"

"We *are* free," Pride said, "and we are choosing to stay."

Ian was confounded by this, not knowing where to start or what to ask. This didn't make any sense. Hundreds of years. Hundreds of years they had been here, and this was their chance to leave. They could do anything. Go anywhere.

Pride continued, "We met, as a group, and decided our work here is not complete. We want to stay on Earth, continuing to help people. We cannot stay in this house any longer, so we bought a new house—"

Evelyn gave a small cough, interrupting him.

"Evelyn bought a house," he corrected.

Ian looked at her, beaming, and she looked back with a sheepish grin.

"Might as well spend my money on something worth having," she said. She reached over and grabbed his hand. "There's a spare room, and we'd like you to move in with us."

All Ian could think was how he could kick himself for how he had acted the past few weeks. The self-loathing and harm and hatred, ready to throw it all away again at the thought of losing everything. But everything he thought he was losing would be right here.

A warmth rose in him for the first time in what felt like years. And just as quickly, it wilted.

They weren't going anywhere, but he was.

"I can't," he breathed.

Evelyn's grip on his hand loosened. He wanted more than anything to tell her to stop. To hold on. To not let go. He didn't want to let go.

"The past four months have been the most interesting of my life. A life that wouldn't be, if it weren't for you," he said, looking up to take the time to meet each of their eyes. "But, it's time I moved on, and it's time someone else gets the help they deserve," he said. "I called my parents and…I told them everything. Well, not everything, not about you all," he quickly corrected, with as much of a smile as he could form, "They know now, what's been happening, and we agreed it would be best if I moved in with them."

The others' faces had fallen. Ian could feel the disappointment in the room, thinly veiled behind masks of hope on everyone's faces. All except one. When Ian met his gaze, he saw Pearce's face shone with pride. Not for himself. Not of ego. Not of self-assuredness, but of happiness.

Six months ago, Ian could have never made that phone call; he would rather have died than ask for help. Pride had known this, of course, outright accused Ian of it—little good that it did. Enough had changed in him now to move back in with his parents at thirty-two years old, and Ian was sure it would look like taking a step back for most people. But now, after all he had been through, it felt like the only path that still led forward.

Ian inclined his head to the creature that first welcomed him to this home, and for the first time, felt he understood him.

"What about not wanting to be a burden on them?" Evelyn asked, a mixture of curiosity and hope that he would change his mind.

Though a small pang went through him at the possibility, at the idea he would be, he knew it was the right decision.

"I'm beginning to learn it's not a burden to let someone love you," he replied, squeezing her hand in return.

Sloth grunted in a way that went higher toward the end.

Louie translated: "Is this goodbye?"

"*No*," Ian rushed. "Not if you'd all…not if it doesn't have to be."

"We will be there," Pride said, almost too quickly. "If you need anything."

"Or just for some advice with the ladies," Louie added with a grin.

Ian didn't know if it was the mood of the evening or the panic that things were changing, but he looked to Louie and asked, "Actually, can I speak to you in your room?"

☩

Lust's room was a faded shell of what it had been just weeks before, the paint and faded outlines of where his furniture once lay being the only indications that he was ever there. Its hollow lifelessness fit the house now, in a way that unnerved Ian. It had been Lust, whether he liked to admit it or not, who added so much life to the house. How quickly it could all be stripped away.

Louie shut the door behind them when he entered. "If you was wanting a last-minute demonstration on how to stuff the clam, I'm sorry to disappoint," he said, gesturing to where the California king bed once lay, "they've taken me canvas."

Ian actually laughed. "Not tonight."

"What'll it be then?" Lust asked.

Even in the dull ache that permeated the evening, in the very room they stood in, the Spirit radiated joy. Ian wrung his hands. He had done this so many times these past months, but found he hadn't grown tired of it. He only wished he had done it sooner. "I owe you an apology and—a thank you," he said.

"For that thing back when? You already did." Lust waved his hands toward him, dismissing the notion.

"No. A real apology," Ian said, trying his hardest to keep his gaze lifted, shifting foot to foot instead. "I treated you like scum for months. Worse than that, even. And you never took shots at me."

"I seem to remember makin' a fair amount of suicide jokes," Lust said. "Funny ones too." He smiled at this apparent statement of fact.

How easy it would be, Ian thought, to lean into Lust's humor and let it go.

"Exactly—jokes. Which is what the thank you is for. I can't imagine it was fun being around me all this time, wallowing and bringing everyone down. You were always a light, though," Ian said. "A distracting light, sometimes, but in every room you walk into, you bring an energy I know I'll never possess, and that makes this all the more difficult. It's the type of thing I never craved, when I didn't know about it, but now that I do, life is going to be a little dimmer."

Lust's mouth dropped and his eyes got wide. "—Are you sayin'?"

"I'm going to miss y—" Ian started but couldn't get the words out before Lust bear-hugged him around the midsection, squeezing the air from his lungs. For such a small man, he was very strong.

"Oh, boyo, I'm gonna miss you too," Lust said, his face pressed into Ian's chest hard enough to cause a pinch.

Not wanting to ruin the moment, Ian decided not to mention it, but that was soon wasted as he felt a hand moving lower.

"You've got a firm ass," Lust said, muffled into his chest. "Been workin' on that with Gavin?"

Ian just pursed his lips and sighed through his nose before letting go of the hug. "Thank you," he said. "I do have one other question."

"Always here to help," Louie said, wiping at his eyes.

"That first month in the house. You mentioned catching me…do something."

"Making the bald man cry?" Lust asked with a straight face.

Ian sighed again, trying not to let the night overwhelm him. "Yes. That."

"What about it?"

"You told me not to think about my ex-wife while doing it. Why?" Ian asked.

To his surprise, Lust smiled.

"Life is about bonds. Bonds with people, mostly. And you build those bonds through time. Sometimes with words, sometimes by just bein' in the same room, sometimes with acts," Lust said, raising his eyebrows. "Every time you touch yourself and think about her, you strengthen that bond. The problem is, you're only strengthenin' it for you."

Ian thought about this for a moment, caught off guard at the straightforward answer. "You know, Evelyn always told me you were a lot wiser than you looked."

"Yes, well, there's that, and the fact that there's billions of cats in the world, why think about the same one if you don't have to?"

Ian laughed again, moving to the door and to rejoin the others. "I knew that was in there somewhere."

Louie gave him a smile he wouldn't soon forget. "Take care, boyo."

☦

The rest of the evening was perhaps the nicest they had ever had together, save for the Gala. Bittersweet. Ian was thankful for the moment, only wishing he could've had it sooner with them. Wishing he had been someone who was capable of it sooner.

He had asked how much longer they would be staying in the rundown old house, and wasn't surprised to find out the Spirits had already been evicted; they had just broke in for the night. Tomorrow they would return to their recently purchased eight-bedroom mansion on the east side. A nicer home than the one they sat in currently, though residing in a despondent neighborhood all the same, one they would have no trouble finding new subjects in.

It turned out they could not wholly relinquish their wicked ways, as Evelyn had agreed to pay for the home on the basis that she had priority in picking who they helped, wanting to focus on abused sex workers. For once, it was a manipulation Ian didn't find issue with.

When the topic turned to him and his future plans, Ian found he had few answers, and was surprised even more at the peace he found in that. He had no interest in continuing his work in private equity, no matter how lucrative he knew it to be, and he still lacked the desire to date. For the first time since the divorce, he knew that had nothing to do with his ex-wife. He'd move in with his parents, find a job doing something he enjoyed, and let the rest work itself out in time. He mostly wanted to focus on the people in his life, a new feeling he quite enjoyed.

When the night was over, he said his goodbyes, knowing it would not be for the last time, and Evelyn walked him to the door.

He was just reaching for the handle when her voice stopped him.

"You've changed," she said.

He turned to look at her. "Is this where you tell me how much better and healthier I look?" Ian joked, but Evelyn didn't laugh.

"You do look healthier, but I was talking about your eyes," she said, reaching up to place a hand on his cheek the same as that day they shared in the park. "They no longer hold what you've lost, only what you want."

And he knew exactly what she meant.

"Don't let the others take too much credit. It was mostly you, you know? I wouldn't be here if it wasn't for you." Ian felt the sting in his eyes ready to overflow down the face she still caressed.

"I know. It'll be our little secret," Evelyn said, straightening up and removing her hand. "When are you moving back home?" she asked.

Ian smiled at her, perhaps his most genuine in memory.

"I am home," he said, before an unfamiliarity pulled his attention away.

Ian looked up from their place in the foyer, a clear shot to the kitchen in view. Over her shoulder, he saw something he never had before.

23

A wide open basement door.

Epilogue

BUSINESS WEEKLY

Time told all. *Two years removed from our article on the local tycoon, Giovanni Costa, the founder and CEO of Mammon Group, is off to prison.*

In April of last year, the businessman, better known as Gio, was indicted on twenty-seven counts of healthcare fraud, insurance fraud, and conspiracy to commit wire fraud, among others. The court documents outline an all-encompassing plan, run by him and his associates, where multiple healthcare claims would be filed under the same person at different hospitals, sometimes years after a patient had been discharged. During the trial, the thirty-eight-year-old maintained claims of innocence, citing no knowledge of the crimes, though the jury's verdict was unanimous.

Gio was taken into custody at 11 a.m. from his corporate office, after failing to self-report. He will serve his seven-year sentence at East Louton Corrections Facility, where recently appointed warden, Wren Bauer, promises a focus on rehabilitation under her new leadership.

Afterword

Thank you so much for being here. Whether you loved it or not, I appreciate your time.

Before we wrap up, there's one note I'd like to add, as I know it will be a topic in reviews. In all the feedback sessions, only one chapter had any consistent negative feedback: chapter 17. About 50% of people didn't like it.

The feedback ranged everything from "It doesn't fit the book" to "It feels like a man showing off that he knows where the clitoris is" (Jokes on you, I know it's a myth).

After speaking with many people, I decided to keep it in.

What I wrote was something that I found plausible for Ian's character, around classes that truly exist, and a scene that deals with one of Ian's core issues- his sexual shame. And ultimately, I found it to be a scene that made many readers as uncomfortable as it made Ian, which is to say, it did exactly as I intended it to.

Thank you again,

-Lyn

Acknowledgments

Somewhere between 2018 and 2020 I decided I would be a writer, and failed at it for many years before taking it seriously. I am eternally selfish in my pursuits, and eternally grateful for the patience of those around me. I know I didn't always make it easy and I'm very grateful to the people who allowed me to be here.

This book in particular is owed to many people.

To Evans and Esther, who let me use their house in Georgia to start this journey.

To Trevor and Jen, who sat with me at a Comic-Con writing panel, and told me I was talented enough to be on it.

To my brothers, Colton and Cameron who never make me feel bad about the heights of my delusional dreams.

To Gina, for reading everything I sent, no matter the hour or inconvenience, and for being my alpha reader.

To my parents, who let me move back in at 27, when I was as lost as ever. For telling me I could do anything in life, and making me believe it. For putting your wants and desires below mine, no matter how many times I begged you not to.

I finished my first book of many, and it was all because of you.

Thank you.